Our Fathers' Lies

Our Fathers' Lies

A Novel of Suspense by
ANDREW TAYLOR

DODD, MEAD & COMPANY
NEW YORK

Copyright © 1985 by Andrew Taylor
All rights reserved
No part of this book may be reproduced in any form
without permission in writing from the publisher.
Published by Dodd, Mead & Company, Inc.
79 Madison Avenue, New York, N.Y. 10016
Manufactured in the United States of America
Designed by Helen Winfield
First Edition

First published in 1985 by Victor Gollancz Ltd., London

Library of Congress Cataloging in Publication Data

Taylor, Andrew, 1951-
Our fathers' lies.

I. Title.
PR6070.A79O9   1985   823'.914   85-10289
ISBN 0-396-08751-5

FOR PENNY

Prologue

Harry lay on his side, picking his nose and waiting. He had drawn back the curtains before switching out the light and getting into bed. As time passed, he found he could distinguish different degrees of darkness. On the opposite wall, for example, were two shadowy oblongs. They represented the chest of drawers and the oak bookcase containing the books that had been his father's. The wallpaper behind them was paler. In the daytime, pink rose rioted there against a cream background spotted with dampstains.

But the ultimate darkness lay beyond the window. He knew what was there: a hemisphere of sky with a base of black mud. He didn't need to see it—he could hear its presence in the gasps of the wind and the vicious spitting of the rain against the windowpane.

If only the storm were louder. It failed to conceal those other, nearer sounds, which came between Harry and sleep. Through the partition wall, he could hear the creak of his aunt's bedsprings. She was moaning again; her gasps were higher-pitched and more regular than those of the wind.

He shivered, despite the warmth of the bedclothes. Two or three years ago, when he was a kid, he would have

1

been beside his aunt in her bed. Even now he had nightmares of drowning in that dry, scented flesh, which seemed to spread over the whole mattress. In those days she hadn't moaned, though she nearly always talked. He remembered it as a tug-of-war with himself as the rope: on the one side was the brightness of the bedside light, the pinches that left bruises on his arm, and the whine of that thin, querulous voice; on the other was the dark warmth of sleep.

Tension knitted his muscles as he waited. Part of him wondered whether events would take their usual course; the rest felt guilty for such detachment. But curiosity, Harry told himself, proper scientific curiosity, was a virtue.

The bedsprings in the next room creaked more loudly. His aunt's footsteps stumbled across the floor. She flung back the mahogany seat of the commode. The retching followed in its appointed place, punctuated with groans.

Then came a silence which was infinitely worse than the retching. It seemed to Harry that his aunt had now merged with the wind, the rain, the Fen landscape, and the blackness.

More footsteps. The shocking sounds of breaking glass— the water jug perhaps? And three heavy thuds on the wall, just above the head of his bed.

Harry allowed himself the luxury of remembering his father. It must have been far worse than this on the Western Front.

"Coming!" His voice cracked: the first syllable was high, the second low. As he sat up in bed he felt his face flushing. He didn't feel he owned his body any more. It had become a traitor, holding its erstwhile master to scorn in the eyes of the world.

The cold enveloped him when he got out of bed. He

2

fumbled across the eiderdown for his dressing gown. Its bulk brought both the promise of future warmth and the familiar sense of present embarrassment. It reached his ankles. The sleeves had been rolled up so they encircled his wrists like padded manacles. *Don't be such a baby, Harry. You'll soon grow into it. It will last you for years . . .*

His feet found his slippers while his hands knotted the dressing-gown cord. He walked across the known darkness of his room, opened the door and slipped out to the landing. The retching began again; this time his own stomach churned in sympathy. He brushed his hand down the wall until it encountered the cold brass dome of the light switch.

The brightness hurt his eyes. It was a crime against the darkness. He knocked on his aunt's door. There was no answer, though the retching had stopped for the time being. He twisted the doorknob and put his head into the room.

Only the pink-shaded lamp by the bed was alight, leaving most of the room in shadows. The stench swept out to greet him. Its pungent, fetid breath defiled him instantly.

Harry covered his mouth and nostrils with his hands. *Worse in the trenches, old man.* He saw his aunt slumped on the carpet, her arms gripping the seat of the open commode. Her nightdress had ridden up, revealing part of a white, bloated thigh, streaked with blue veins. Harry swallowed. His gaze traveled up the stained nightdress to his aunt's face. Her gray, greasy hair, usually confined to a bun, straggled down to her shoulders. The face itself was gaunt; only the sagging cheeks preserved the memory of former plumpness. The skin looked green and waxen.

3

"Get Bea . . ."

Harry saw the lips move but the sound itself seemed to have come from someone else. It was not a voice he recognized.

The head swung back to the commode and Harry jerked out of the room, banging the door behind him in his haste. He ran down the stairs to the first-floor landing and knocked on the door of the bedroom where Aunt Bea and Uncle John slept. There was no answer. He knocked again, wondering if he should go in but afraid of how Uncle John would react.

A loud wail issued through the open door of the adjacent room. Oh God, he had awakened Cousin George.

But the baby's cries were immediately effective. Aunt Bea stood in the doorway, smoothing down the white lace at the front of her nightdress. The light was on. Harry could see Uncle John sitting up in bed. His face was red and wore an unexpectedly petulant expression, like that of a spoilt child who had just been deprived of a treat.

"What is it?" snapped Aunt Bea as she pushed by Harry and went into George's room. For once the wailing stopped and George slipped back into sleep. "Well?"

Harry felt himself the focus of two angry gazes—Uncle John's from the bed and Aunt Bea's from the doorway of George's room. The injustice goaded him into raising his voice above a whisper.

"It's Aunt Muriel. She's having another of her attacks—worse than I've ever seen her. She wants you to go to her."

"Well, don't just stand there, Harry. Go to the kitchen, make up the range and put on the big kettle."

"Go on, boy." Uncle John's voice was heavy and husky. "I'll be down in a moment to give you a hand."

4

Harry went downstairs. As always at night, the ground floor looked both strange and familiar, like an untenanted scene in a recurring dream. He moved mechanically down the hallway to the kitchen. The routine took over. It was always the same when Aunt Muriel—*the* Aunt, as Harry thought of her—had one of her attacks: tea, hot-water bottles, towels, and clean sheets; the two aunts engaged in hushed feminine ministrations behind closed doors; and Uncle John prowling through the house in search of an outlet for his suppressed energy.

Ten minutes later Uncle John appeared in the kitchen. He was wearing a red silk dressing gown and smoking a cigarette. He made no attempt at conversation, but paced up and down as Harry laid the tea tray.

"A cup for you, Uncle?"

Uncle John stopped and stared down at the tray. There were four cups. He jabbed an orange-stained forefinger toward them.

"You know who has what?"

"Yes, Uncle. You have white with two sugars; Aunt Bea's with lemon; Aunt Muriel has black with three sugars when she's like this."

"Probably won't be able to keep it down, in her state." Uncle John sounded as if he was talking to himself. He looked down at Harry, his black, long-lashed eyes hard and bright. "I'll take the tray up. You get on with the bottles. Bloody woman."

It was after two o'clock by the time Harry got back to bed. His hot-water bottle was cold. The wind had died down; the blackness outside was calm but no less menacing; condensation had made strange shapes on the window, like gray faces peering in.

Next door he could hear murmuring. The moans had

5

stopped. Despite cold feet and hands, Harry fell asleep almost immediately. He dreamed that the gray faces had come into the room and floated round the bed, mocking him. Only two held back, remaining by the fireplace. Harry craned his head toward them but could not make out their features. He knew they must belong to his father and mother.

Breakfast in the morning was a silent meal. Neither of the aunts was there. The little maid who came in during the day asked when the mistress would be down and what she should do about luncheon.

Uncle John put down his paper. "Miss Hinton will have some sort of invalid pap in her room, I imagine. Mrs. Landis will be down for lunch; and I'll be in today as well. That's all."

The maid bobbed a token curtsy and left the room.

"What about me?" Harry asked. There was a hint of panic in his voice. Sometimes people seemed to forget his existence. He had a secret fear that, if everyone forgot at the same time, he would no longer be there.

"Oh yes. Your aunt and I have decided it would be best for you to go to your grandmother's for a few days. Aunt Muriel's having a bad go of it this time. We might even have to get a nurse in. God knows what that will cost . . . in any case, if we do, she'll need your room. I'll telephone the village taxi after breakfast. You'd better pack a few things, I suppose. Try not to bother your aunt. She's fagged out after last night."

"Must I, Uncle? I—"

"Don't fuss, boy. You're better out of the way. Better for all concerned."

❀   ❀   ❀

Three days later Harry was released from his grandmother's tyranny in that crowded house in Barnes. The taxi was there to meet him at Ely station. Stokes the driver said nothing as Harry slid into the seat beside him. They drove in silence through the rain, which blanketed the Fens.

As they pulled up outside the house, the front door opened. Uncle John emerged, bearing the unusual courtesy of an umbrella. He was wearing a black armband. Harry's eyes glanced away from it on to the facade of the house. All the blinds were down. The windows were closed eyes, wet with the rain. On cue, Harry felt his own eyes fill with tears.

Stokes touched Harry's shoulder, a gesture that was half an invitation to get out of his car and half an unexpectedly reassuring pat. "Poor kid," he said. "I thought they would have told you."

1

MAJOR DOUGAL STEPPED from the crematorium chapel into the sunlight. He avoided the other mourners, who were tending to cluster around the two hired Rolls Royces, and stared over the neat lawns and primly regimented flower beds. The place looked like a municipal park, not a place of death, just as the chapel was more like a serious-minded village hall than a place of worship. It was impossible to believe that Richard Prentisse's mortal remains had been in that wooden box, which had vanished, like a conjurer's illusion, behind the red velvet curtain. The service was partly to blame: both the colorless modern liturgy and the studiously undenominational clergyman had conspired to deny death its primacy. Death had been sanitized; and Major Dougal felt the poorer for it.

"Sad business, Ted. You'd known him a long time?"

Major Dougal turned. He wondered how the curate came to be so free with his Christian name.

"Since the war. He was in my company. Never lost touch afterward. Godfathers to one another's children. You know the sort of thing."

"Quite, quite." The curate scratched his large brown beard. "Still, it was a mercifully quick way to go."

Major Dougal was tempted to ask where Richard had

gone. But this sort of clergyman wouldn't have any hard information on the subject. Modern theological colleges must train their alumni to be vague, on the grounds that certainties would only confuse or alienate their future flocks of unbelievers.

"Uncle Ted?" The Major turned to find Celia Prentisse at his elbow. She was wearing a black suit and had her blond hair scraped back. Her eyes were huge behind the dark rims of her glasses.

"Hullo, my dear."

"You will let me know if there's anything I can do, Celia?" The curate backed away, leaving the Major alone with his goddaughter.

"Margaret's laid on a sort of buffet lunch. She wants to know if you're coming."

"Would you mind if I didn't? I hate these gatherings." Major Dougal thought that Celia would know the real reason: Margaret, her stepmother, had only asked him from a sense of duty; she had never approved of her husband's friends who belonged to the period before their marriage.

"No, of course not. I wish I didn't have to go either. She's got out the best china and terrorized the char. You know, it's the state banquet treatment."

"Perhaps it's her way of coping."

"You don't believe that and nor do I. You should see her when the solicitor told her about the mortgage. It was one of those endowment schemes—now Daddy's dead it's automatically paid off and the house belongs outright to Margaret. She's already talking about selling it and buying a villa in Portugal . . . Oh, I'm sorry, Uncle Ted, I—"

Celia broke off, found a handkerchief in her handbag and blew her nose. Major Dougal took her arm.

"Your father would have wanted her to be happy."

9

Celia looked up at him. "Death brings out the worst in people, doesn't it? The one who's dead just vanishes. Sweep him under the carpet, grab the possessions and run. I feel guilty for spending more time loathing Margaret than mourning Daddy."

Major Dougal stared at the black, mirrorlike surface of his toe caps. Privately he thought that mourning the dead was always difficult: it was much easier to hate the living.

"You're not much help." Celia nearly managed a smile, which took the edge off her words. "I suppose nobody can be."

Her eyes filled with tears, magnified by her glasses. Embarrassment swept over Major Dougal.

"You will let me know," he blurted, "if there's anything I can do. I mean it."

"There is, actually. I wanted to have a chat. I thought if you were coming to the lunch . . ."

"What about?"

"I just need someone to tell me I'm being stupid. I—I keep imagining things about Daddy. Could I come around and see you?"

"Of course. Any time."

"Perhaps tomorrow morning?"

"All right. But I should warn you—"

"Celia!"

Celia said softly, "Damn."

"The car's waiting, dear." Margaret Prentisse seized her stepdaughter by the arm as if she was an errant handbag. "Ted. How kind. Are you coming back with us?"

"Thank you but no, Margaret. I was just—"

Mrs. Prentisse's smile flashed in farewell. "We must love you and leave you. There's so much to *do*."

"Good-bye, Uncle Ted." Celia's voice was coldly formal. She inclined a cheek toward him for a kiss.

10

Major Dougal took the hint: the visit she had proposed was not to be discussed in Margaret's presence. He watched as the two black figures were swallowed by the big black car. He glanced over his shoulder, half afraid he would see a chimney wafting the mortal remains of Richard into the still autumn air. Of course not. The crematorium was far too tasteful.

It was a pity that he had been unable to warn Celia. Still, he was probably being ridiculously oversensitive on her account. After all, she had other things on her mind.

2

THE MORNING AFTER the funeral was drowsy, sunny, and oppressively dull. Celia got up late and sat in the kitchen in front of a pot of coffee. She had taken the whole week off work and now felt slightly guilty about it: there was nothing she could do at home.

The neatness of the kitchen reproached her. All traces of yesterday's jamboree had been swept away. A Hoover purred in the sitting room; it was Friday, so Mrs. Gann would be here—she came and did on Tuesday and Friday mornings, as well as by arrangement on special occasions like yesterday.

The Hoover stopped, and the sound of conversation filtered through to the kitchen. Mrs. Gann would be in her classic pose for talking—one hand holding the duster while the other restrained the Hoover; she treated the vacuum cleaner as if it was a restive horse and never relaxed until it was safely stabled under the stairs.

Her father's spare glasses were still on the kitchen mantelpiece. The corners of the case were frayed. Celia picked them up and wished she could throw them away. That, unfortunately, was Margaret's job. She put them out of sight behind the clock. Just another of death's loose ends.

The door opened.

"Oh, hullo," Margaret said. She was wearing a blue housecoat and looked as sparkling as her kitchen. "Up at last?"

Mrs. Prentisse fetched a cup and saucer from the draining board, sat down at the table and poured herself some coffee.

"Silence is so restful," she remarked. Her hands deftly rounded up the crumbs on the table from Celia's toast and deposited them on her plate. "I don't think Mrs. Gann has stopped talking since she got here."

With you listening avidly, you old hag.

"She enjoyed yesterday, of course. That gave her something to talk about. Other people's relatives are always so interesting to that class of person. And as a bonus her George went to the Angel last night and you know what he's like. A perfect *sponge* for gossip."

In response to an unspoken request, Celia passed her stepmother the sugar.

"Thank you, dear. I really must try saccharin again. The trouble is, it tastes so awful. But Doctor Haines said some dreadful things about sugar . . . where was I?"

"George at the Angel."

"Oh yes. You'll never guess who he saw there last night." Margaret paused.

Celia obediently prompted: "Who?"

"A returning prodigal." Margaret sipped her coffee with the daintiness of a sparrow at a birdbath. "William Dougal!"

Celia said nothing. She had learned long ago that with her stepmother silence was the best policy. She had a vivid mental image of herself standing on the table and brandishing her fist in the general direction of God.

13

Couldn't He at least leave a decent interval between the catastrophes He prescribed for her?

"There. I thought that would interest you." Margaret smiled complacently. "Apparently he was as bold as brass. I know it was ten years ago, but you'd think he'd have the decency not to flaunt himself. People have long memories in little places like this."

"Is . . . is he staying with Uncle Ted?"

"So it seems. Poor man. He may be deadly dull, but he didn't deserve a son like that. I could never understand what you and your father saw in him; William, I mean."

Celia reined in her anger. "Maybe there were mitigating circumstances. We don't know the full story."

"I doubt it." Margaret pursed her lips, ruining the carefully made-up prettiness of her doll-like face. "Even as a teenager he was sly. Butter wouldn't melt in his mouth. And that school of his expelled him or something, didn't it? I told your father he should put his foot down about you seeing so much of him. What happened came as no surprise to me, I can tell you."

"No," said Celia evenly, "I don't suppose it did." She pushed back her chair and got up. "I won't be in for lunch, by the way."

"You will remember about your father's papers, won't you? I don't ask much, but as you know—"

"I'll make a start this afternoon."

"Not the financial files, of course. But I would be grateful if you would go through his research files. It's sad, but you must be ruthless. We can't afford to be sentimental. But put any finished work on one side—his publisher might be interested. Not that I think there's likely to be anything. As you know, he was between books when he died. You'll find the black plastic sacks in the scullery on the bottom left-hand shelf."

14

"Okay."

"And then there's the books. At least they should be worth something. They certainly ought to, with the amount he spent on them. Your father never seemed to appreciate the *space* they took up. Not everyone likes living in a library. He bought a whole carload a few weeks before he died. Such a waste."

"Is that when he bought the encyclopedia? I hadn't seen that before."

"That huge pile of black books in the corner by the desk? That upset me, I don't mind telling you. You know they're seventy or eighty years old. Totally useless. I said, 'If you're throwing money away, I could do with a new fridge-freezer.' But he was over the moon about them."

"Probably they were useful for his work." Celia felt perversely determined to remind her stepmother who had paid the bills. "Look, I'll try and go through the books before I go home on Sunday. A few might be worth selling separately—the antiquarian stuff. Otherwise we might as well get someone in to make an offer for the rest as a job lot. Do you mind if I take a few for myself?"

Margaret paused just long enough to make her acquiescence seem grudging. She nodded. "Of course. Your father would have wanted it. You'd better make a list of any other bits and bobs you'd like."

Celia moved toward the door. "Anything I can get you while I'm in town?"

"No thank you, dear. I'll be going myself this afternoon. You've still got your own key, haven't you? I doubt if I'll be back before six or seven. I said I'd have tea with Mrs. Grimes and you know what she's like when she get's going."

That makes two of you.

"Right," said Celia aloud. "See you this evening."

15

"Be good, dear," Margaret said vaguely; and then in a sharper voice she added an impossible rider: "Don't do anything I wouldn't do."

It was a relief to be out of the house. Major Dougal lived on the other side of town, about a mile away. Celia decided against taking the car.

The walk soothed her by its familiarity: it was like strolling through childhood. Plumford occupied a shallow bowl bisected by the sluggish meandering of the river. Her route took her down the gentle hill into the broad market street. At one end was the gray flint tower of the parish church; at the other was the soft red brick of the old town hall, an ornate yet oddly domestic building in the Dutch style. There were faces she knew among the passersby, but to her relief no one stopped to talk to her.

She found her mind running more on William than on what she wanted to discuss with the Major. It must be ten years since she had seen him: quite time enough to be purged the pain from her memories of him. Besides, she was living with Jim now, with the prospect of marriage looming increasingly large in the future.

Nevertheless, she was pleased that she had washed her hair this morning, and that the slight autumn nip in the air justified her wearing her leather coat. She had made both decisions before hearing that William was back. The only consequence of the news of his arrival was that she had spent a few minutes more on her makeup than she would have done for the Major alone. That was allowable on grounds of self-respect: you couldn't let an old boyfriend think you'd retreated into purdah since his departure.

16

Major Dougal's bungalow was in what Mrs. Prentisse called the wrong end of Plumford. By this she meant it was fringed by council estates and within hearing range of the railway. The bungalow looked tattier than usual. The paint on the front gate and on the outside woodwork of the house was peeling; several slates hung crookedly on the roof; the rust spots on the Ford Anglia in the drive seemed more extensive than before; and the small garden looked as if its long-term plan was to smother the house it encircled.

Celia rang the doorbell, and suddenly her brittle self-confidence shattered like toffee tapped by a mallet. What on earth was she doing, wantonly risking a confrontation with William Dougal at a time like this? God knew she felt fragile enough as it was.

The door opened, leaving no more time for the luxury of panic. Memory adjusted to present reality like a camera lens coming into focus.

"Hullo, William," she said. "You're looking well."

He leaned forward and, before she could recoil, kissed her on the cheek. It was neatly done; Celia remembered that William, unlike Jim, had always been adept at avoiding her glasses on these occasions.

"How nice to see you. I was very sorry to hear about Uncle Richard. If I'd known sooner I'd have liked to come to the funeral. Come on in."

He stood against the wall to allow Celia to slip by him into the dark, narrow hall. His hair was much shorter than it had been, emphasizing the gauntness of his face; and he had shaved. In the old days his chin always seemed to be blue with stubble. He was wearing jeans and a cream shirt that looked suspiciously like silk. He was as enviably skinny as he had been as an adolescent.

17

Celia stumbled against the hatstand, abruptly cutting short her comparisons with the past.

"Sorry," William said. "I should have put the light on. Can I take your coat? My father's in the sitting room."

"No I'm not." Major Dougal appeared in the kitchen doorway. "How are you, my dear?"

"Fine." Celia shrugged herself out of her coat, trying not to appear as clumsy as she felt. "I hope this isn't an inconvenient time for you. I heard through Mrs. Gann that William was back."

"Not at all," said the Major firmly.

"I thought I might go and mow the lawn," William remarked to nobody in particular.

"Not for my sake." Celia looked at Major Dougal. "William knew Daddy too. And as he hasn't seen him for so long, perhaps he can be more objective than we can."

"It's up to you, my dear. But let's go and sit down. Do you want some coffee? Or a drink?"

Celia shook her head. She led the way into the sitting room. It was a long room, running the length of the bungalow, with a bay window at one end and a wall full of books at the other. It was shabby but meticulously clean. On the shelf above the gas fire was a black-and-white photograph of a laughing woman, enclosed in a silver frame. Celia could just remember Aunt Anne.

It was a room full of memories: her father and Uncle Ted arguing fiercely about military technicalities of the Crimean War, pulling books from the shelves to illustrate their points; she (adoring) and William (disdainful) playing Monopoly in the corner by the window, on that part of the Axminster where the Chinese pattern of the nap had worn down to a soft, silvery blur; and later, she and

William white-faced on the sofa, trying to escape from a trap they had somehow built around themselves.

When they were seated there was an awkward pause. Celia didn't want to break the silence: after all, what response could she expect but the usual masculine patronage, bland and ineffectual. William sat perfectly still on the sofa, as alert as a cat in repose. Major Dougal tugged at the knees of his tweed trousers in a reflex attempt to preserve their creases. Finally, he ran his fingers through his bushy white hair and cleared his throat.

"Time we began. What's worrying you?"

Celia asked: "What does William know about how Daddy died?"

"I don't know," said the Major gruffly. "We haven't talked about it." Father and son glanced briefly at one another in a way that suggested there was quite a lot they hadn't talked about.

"I heard something in the Angel last night." William touched his hair in a disconcerting mirror image of his father's gesture. "They said he was drowned somewhere near Dunwich; and that the coroner's verdict was suicide. You see, my father was out shopping when I got here yesterday—that's why I first heard the news in the pub."

Celia stared at the photograph of Aunt Anne. "Margaret was out at work on the day he died. When she got back in the evening he wasn't in and the car wasn't there. That didn't disturb her—he quite often goes—went—out in the early evening for a drink or a walk, especially in summer. She started to get worried about nine and rang all the places he might be—me, Doctor Haines, Uncle Ted, a few pubs, and so on. I rang the local hospitals and, when he hadn't come home by midnight, the police. They were very soothing—apparently hundreds of peo-

19

ple go missing every week, and most of them turn up un-harmed sooner rather than later. The next morning they found the car. It was parked off the road in a bit of wood-land between Walberswick and Dunwich. The next thing we knew, some kid on holiday had found his clothes about a quarter of a mile away on the beach."

She stopped and looked at the Dougals. "I gave up hope then. I knew we wouldn't find him alive."

"Why were you so sure?" asked William quietly.

"Something had to be badly wrong because he was acting so out of character. He was never exactly the out-door type—I can't remember him going swimming since I was about five. And anyway he was very prudish: *all* his clothes were there. If he'd had a sudden urge to so swim-ming, he'd have kept on his underpants at least."

"Not if he wasn't quite himself at the time." The Major lowered his voice. "The other evidence did—um—sug-gest . . ."

Celia took a deep breath and, as her father had always advised her to do in moments of stress, counted slowly and inwardly to five. She should have known the Dougals would be *reasonable;* just like Margaret, Doctor Haines and the police.

William deflected the conversation. "How about his pockets? Was everything there?"

She turned to him in relief. "Yes. His wallet—with quite a lot of cash. House and car keys. And the usual clutter he always carried around: penknife, bits of string, a couple of safety pins, a notebook, a biro—he was a reg-ular boy scout, my father. Be prepared. There . . . there was also a bottle of gin, half-drunk, and a paperback se-lection of Schopenhauer's essays and aphorisms."

William laughed. "The gin sounds like Uncle Richard.

20

But Schopenhauer? He must have changed. He used to despise philosophy. I remember arguing with him about it. He'd always end up saying—"

"Philosophy, as Chesterfield said of idleness,"—Celia's imitation of the voice her father assumed in tipsily pedantic moments was uncannily accurate—*"is only the refuge of weak minds."*

They smiled at one another while Major Dougal once more raked his hair back and cleared his throat. Celia's smile faded.

"He hadn't changed. What made it even stranger was that the book was open at the essay on suicide."

"Schopenhauer justifies it, doesn't he?"

"In so many words. He argues that there's no moral reason to condemn suicide—that Christianity makes it a crime for religious reasons. Daddy had marked the bit at the end—something about the physical pain of death losing significance in the face of spiritual suffering."

"Doesn't sound like the Richard I knew," said the Major unwillingly. "It was his book, I suppose? And he had marked that particular passage?"

"It was just a line in ink in the margin. The ink was the same as the biro he carried—a blue Parker. As for the book, I'd never seen it; but there was no reason why I should have done. I've not been living in the same house for years. Margaret didn't recognize it but then she never looks at books. It was a Penguin, well-worn, with "30p" pencilled on the flyleaf. He could have bought it anywhere. You know what he was like about secondhand bookshops."

Major Dougal frowned. "If he didn't like philosophy, why should he buy it?"

"It might have been for background detail. One of the

21

last things he did was an article on von Kleist for one of the Sunday magazines." She noticed a flicker of bewilderment on the Major's face. "He was a German romantic who committed suicide with his mistress sometime in the eighteen hundreds."

"In 1811, I think," said William with an apologetic grimace. "It's feasible, I suppose. They were contemporaries, give or take a decade or so."

Celia shook her head violently. Why did he have to be so calmly academic? "What does it matter? Even if Daddy did want it for research, it doesn't explain why he killed himself. He *despised* suicide, I tell you. A friend of mine at college killed herself just before finals. I rang Daddy expecting to get sympathy; all I got was this spiel about life being our most priceless gift, and how wrong it was to throw it away."

"Perhaps something had happened to change his mind," said the Major cautiously. "It does happen. There was a chap in my regiment: bright, breezy and intensely Christian type. Then he had a letter from his wife saying she'd—hum—been unfaithful. He blew his brains out in the lavatory, poor man."

"Yes, but *what* could have happened?" Celia realized she was almost shouting, more by the way the men were looking at her than by the sound. "Look," she continued more quietly, "he wasn't about to die of some agonizing disease. Doctor Haines made that quite clear. He hadn't any money troubles—well, no more than usual. The poor lamb was used to being financially precarious. And he was quite happy with Margaret. I hate to admit it, but she did make him a good wife: she bossed him around for a bit of the time and left him alone for the rest, which was just what he wanted. I talked on the phone to him a couple of days before he vanished, and he was really *bouncy*. In one of his Tigger moods."

Major Dougal nodded. "I saw him in town on the Saturday before. For what it's worth, he seemed pretty cheery to me."

"It was the new book," Celia said. "You know the way he was when an idea was getting hold of him. Before he got down to the slog of researching and writing."

"What was the book going to be about?" William asked.

Celia shrugged. "Nobody knows. Don't you remember his famous theory of creativity? That if you told someone what you were going to write, the act of talking satisfied the urge to communicate; so you never would write it. He even felt dubious about sending outlines to his agent and publisher."

"He didn't send off an outline this time?"

"No, I rang them up and checked. I can't see anything in his study either. There might be something—I've not been through all his papers. I don't think it had reached the point where he needed to put it on paper. It was the part he liked best: that's another reason why he wouldn't have killed himself."

Major Dougal slowly stood up. Celia thought the lines on his face were deeper than usual and wished she hadn't come. She had no right to disturb Uncle Ted. His hand strayed toward the photograph and brushed against the frame; it was an automatic gesture, like touching wood. "Let's have some sherry," he said. "You will stay to lunch, won't you?"

Celia nodded. "You don't believe me," she said flatly. "You think I should mourn Daddy and come to terms with the idea that he killed himself."

The Major looked down at her. "Celia. I'm glad you came. But you have to accept that we never know anyone completely. I wouldn't have thought your father was likely to kill himself either. But on the evidence, we were wrong. Nothing you've said changes that. As you know, I couldn't go to the inquest but I did have a chat with Bob Haines afterwards. There was nothing about your father's death that could be construed as sinister. Surprising, yes. But death always is."

"What about the gin?"

"How do you mean?"

"The bottle on the beach was a supermarket's own brand. But Daddy was a snob about gin. If he'd wanted a little alcoholic comfort in his last moments, do you really think he'd have settled for anything other than Gordon's?"

3

R ICHARD PRENTISSE'S STUDY was on the first floor—a thin, low room with a sloping ceiling. Twenty years ago he had made an abortive attempt to strip the paint from the beams that ran down to the windows: they were now a blotchy patchwork of white paint and bare wood. Books filled the walls from floor to ceiling and took up a sizeable proportion of the floor as well. Between the windows was a large, stained kitchen table, flanked by gray filing cabinets. The tabletop, unlike the rest of the room, was immaculately tidy. On it stood an electric typewriter, a box of paper, an angle-poise lamp, an old cocoa tin containing pens and pencils and three shallow cardboard boxes, marked IN, OUT and GOD KNOWS. Only the last of these had anything in it.

"It feels sacrilegious," Celia said. "If Daddy were going to come back and haunt anywhere, he'd choose this room."

William Dougal, who was standing by the window smoking a cigarette, said nothing. Celia leafed through the contents of the GOD KNOWS tray.

"Bills, mainly," she said. "And an invitation to do an American lecture tour on aspects of nineteenth-century history. I suppose we should give the bills to the executor. Did your father mind?"

William turned his head. "Us coming here? I think he was relieved. It let him off the hook. It got me out of his way, too. He's not quite sure what he should say to me."

"That's hardly surprising, considering he's only seen you about twice in the last ten years." Celia's tone was tart: after all, William still had a father to see.

"You know why that is."

"Perhaps it's about time he did as well . . . Oh hell, I'm sorry. It's just been a bit of a shock to find you in Plumford, on top of everything else. What made you come back?"

William shrugged. "Nostalgia? A bit of guilt? I don't know. I'm between jobs; I needed a rest; it seemed like a good idea at the time. And I wondered how you were—it was hardly something I could ask my father."

Damn him. Celia picked up the topmost bill and pretended to study it. He could have contacted her any time in the last ten years, and he knew it. He must have changed in the last decade—she could feel that he had— even if his waistline hadn't.

"Someone said you were doing another degree," she remarked to the British Telecom bill in her hand.

William grinned. "I did start an M.Phil. a couple of years ago. On pagan Latin literary texts and Charlemagne's court. But that petered out after six months."

"So what are you doing now?"

"I told my father I'm a self-employed antique dealer, but that makes it sound rather grander than it is. I go to auctions in the provinces and sell the stuff in London. Mainly through street markets."

He's lying. Celia was less surprised by this than by the fact that she was still able to tell. It was a faculty she could do without. Jim never told lies, she thought irrelevantly.

26

She felt William's eyes on her and looked up. He had that amused, slightly superior expression on his face that had always riled her. "And?" she challenged. "What else do you do?"

"This and that." The amusement faded from his face. William opened the window and flicked his cigarette butt onto the gravel path beneath. "Shall we start? Margaret might get back early."

Something illegal, I'll bet; he always had an amoral streak in him. But Celia allowed him to change the subject. After all, he had a point. She looked round the cluttered room. "I wish we knew what we were looking for."

"As I see it, we're looking for loose ends. If Uncle Richard didn't commit suicide, he must have died by accident—or someone must have killed him. All we can do is go back over the last few days of his life and look for something that doesn't fit into the usual pattern."

"His diary." Celia pulled open the drawer in the middle of the table and took out a slim black book. "The police returned it with the rest of his things. I had a quick glance at it."

She laid it on the table and switched on the light. William came to stand by her; her body was treacherously conscious of his proximity. The diary was twice as tall as it was wide—the "executive" style, designed to fit in a jacket pocket. She began to turn the pages, hurrying through the earlier months of the year. Each double page showed a full month, with a single line for each day. It was not the sort of diary to which you confided your innermost thoughts. The left-hand page was in general reserved for appointments. *Dentist 10, Lon Lib comm mtg 2.30, Lunch with Charles,* and so on. The right-hand page held another type of entry: *Day rtn London £12.00, Paper £4.25, Taxi £3.50, Photocopying £8.25.*

"Expenses," Celia said. "His accountant made him jot down everything. Daddy hated it."

She paged through to the month of August. Her father had died on the twenty-third, so three full weeks had been used. In the weeks following that date only a sprinkling of entries occurred. Most of them were self-explanatory—an appointment for a dental checkup, the date the car's MOT was due, the renewal of insurance premiums, and Margaret's birthday in November.

"Go back to August," William said. "Who's Charles?"

"Daddy's agent. They had lunch exactly a week before he disappeared. More social than business, I gather. Daddy was in town for the London Library committee meeting."

The last entry was for the twenty-first. Mr. Prentisse had spent a total of £23.85 on his train and tube fares and his lunch. He had again visited the London Library. The rest of the page was blank, except for a few words scrawled at the bottom in the space for memoranda.

Celia said doubtfully, "It looks like *med to mum 481,* except that's nonsense. Both my grandmothers have been dead for years."

"Did he ever call Margaret 'Mum'?"

"No. He wouldn't call anyone Mum if he could help it. It wasn't a word he used. 'Mummy,' perhaps, but not 'Mum.' "

"*Med,*" said William slowly. "Medicine, Mediterranean, *in medias res,* medium, medieval . . . Got any ideas?"

"No. Unless the number is a telephone number. Some of the local ones are still three figures."

The telephone was on the windowsill beside them. Celia picked up the receiver and dialed. It rang three times.

"Pridley Petfoods, can I help you," inquired a breathless voice of indeterminate gender.

"My name's Prentisse. Celia Prentisse. My father just died and I'm clearing up his estate. There's a chance he may have done some business with you recently. Richard Prentisse."

"Don't recall anyone of that name. Of course it's hard to know if they pay cash. I could have a look at our invoice book. Hold on."

There was a pause. "She's checking," Celia said. Then: "What sort of pet did he have?"

"None at all. I suppose he might have bought something for someone else."

"No Prentisse here. Sorry. Not in the last couple of months."

"Sorry to trouble you. Thanks for your help." Celia put down the receiver and looked at William. "This is hopeless."

He was flicking through the earlier months in the diary. "The London Library is funded by members' subscriptions, isn't it? Where is it? He was always going there."

"It's in St. James's Square. Daddy was on the committee. Oh God, that's someone else to write to."

"I wonder if he got anything out last time he went."

Celia stared round the book-filled room. "If he did, we'll never find it."

In the event it took them ten minutes. It was on a small side table, partially obscured by the columns of encyclopedias that towered around it. There was only one book: a small volume with yellowing pages, bound in faded maroon cloth. The author was J. Archibald Owen; the title was *Murder by Stealth: Great Arsenic Cases Over the Centuries.*

*   *   *

They were still arguing about the book the next morning, as Celia's battered Deux Chevaux bore them down the motorway toward London. The fine weather had broken: it was a wet, gusty day. Beyond the arcs of the wipers, the little Citroën's windscreen was brown and murky with the spray thrown up by other traffic. The weather was being how Celia was feeling.

"It's a *sign,*" she insisted for the third time in the last half hour. "It has to be. He knew someone was poisoning him."

"It's very unlikely." William was in the passenger seat, staring at the "No Smoking" sticker, which Celia had stuck just below the road tax disc on the windscreen. "If someone had been poisoning him beforehand, you'd have noticed. There'd be vomiting and diarrhea and things like that. And everyone says he was so cheerful in his last week or so. And if someone gave him a massive dose on the day he died, he wouldn't have known about it beforehand. So why would he have got the book? Anyway, if he thought he was being poisoned, he wouldn't have got a popular collection of case histories; he'd have wanted something more technical. Damn it, he'd have gone to the police or Doctor Haines."

"Crime is a long way outside his usual field."

"True," William conceded. "It was usually nineteenth-century history, wasn't it? And military, police and/or literary. Maybe he got the book purely for pleasure. Or as background for a crime novel."

Celia snorted.

"You never know," William continued patiently. "People do get sudden urges to write crime novels."

The conversation died for want of new material. Celia

drove automatically, trying to avoid thinking of her immediate response to the book's title: *Margaret killed him.* It was the one thing she hadn't mentioned to William; he probably knew what was in her mind, so why bother?

She thought about the book itself. It was something of a period piece: it had been published in 1933, and J. Archibald Owen devoted a good deal of space to vigorous denunciations of the murderers who made his royalties possible. He was not a man who had much time for mitigating circumstances.

He dealt with a couple of dozen cases, beginning with the Marquise de Brinvilliers in France in 1676. Many of them were vaguely familiar to Celia—Mary Blandy, Madeleine Smith, and Florence Maybrick; others, like Dr. King, John Landis, and Major Armstrong, were not. Women seemed to get all the publicity, which was only to be expected in this lip-smacking, male-dominated world.

"Arsenic," William said, "leaves a lot of traces—in the hair and nails, for example. I don't think it's a very fashionable poison these days. I looked it up in that old *Britannica* of your father's. Did you know that when it's vaporized it turns a golden yellow color and smells of garlic?"

The amusement in his voice cost Celia her temper. She swung the Citroën into the center lane, straining to overtake an articulated lorry. A gigantic coach muscled its way into the fast lane. The little car swayed between the juggernauts.

"I feel like the filling in a mobile sandwich." William was gripping his seat belt like a lifeline. "I'm sorry about the garlic."

❁   ❁   ❁

The London Library nestled in the northwest corner of St. James's Square, its Victorian facade looking decidedly drab beside those of its eighteenth-century neighbors. Celia led the way up the steps into the hall. She had sometimes come here with her father, and the building had something of the reassurance of familiar territory. She approached the long, thin assistant behind the long, thin issue-desk on the left of the hall.

"May I see the Librarian-in-charge? My name's Prentisse; my father's on the committee."

A smile spread across the acne-dappled face of the assistant as he took in Celia's appearance. It was meant to be a lecherous look, but its owner's innocence made it offensive.

"The Librarian himself is off duty today." His voice was at least five years older than his face. "Miss Winters is the senior person in the building. She's the Deputy Librarian. Will she do?"

Miss Winters saw them in her office on the ground floor. She was a slender, dark-haired woman in her thirties with a long jaw and a large nose. She wore no jewelry except an eighteenth-century mourning ring on the third finger of her right hand.

"We were so sorry to hear about your father," she said to Celia. "We saw it in the *Telegraph*. We shall miss him—unlike some of our committee members, he didn't treat the staff as an automatic retrieval system on legs." A smile curved across her thin, sallow face. "And he could be wonderfully ruthless with time-wasters. I wish we had more like him."

"Yes . . . " Celia could think of nothing more to say. William wasn't much help: he was slumped in the hard chair beside her, his legs crossed, examining the spines of

32

a trolley-load of shiny new volumes. He would probably start reading one soon.

"Was there anything . . . ?" Miss Winters inquired delicately.

Celia delved into her bag and put *Murder by Stealth* on Miss Winters's desk. "I wanted to return this," she said. "It was the only London Library Book I could see at home. Perhaps you'd let me know if he had anything else out."

Miss Winters smiled in acknowledgment and crossed her arms over her chest. She wanted more, Celia realized: at a time like this no one would bother to come up from Suffolk on a personal visit when there was a perfectly good postal service in existence.

"My father's agent," Celia went on, "wanted to know what he was working on when he died. We can't find any notes at home. I wondered if you might have an idea."

Miss Winters said nothing for a moment. Celia thought her dark eyes were staring through the transparency of a lie; after all, why should the agent want to know in what direction Mr. Prentisse's work was going?

"He spent a morning here," the librarian said at last, "a couple of days before he died. I talked with him myself, as a matter of fact. He was interested in two things, one of which puzzled me a little—it was outside his usual interests. He consulted some old Army Lists. That was normal enough. But he was also looking for information on the Landis case."

"Landis?" William said suddenly. "One of the cases here?" His index finger tapped twice on the cover of *Murder by Stealth*.

"That's right. We weren't much use to him, I'm afraid. The murder doesn't seem to have attracted much cover-

33

age. Just a few references here and there. J. Archibald Owen's account was the longest we could find."

"It happened between the wars," William said. "The newspapers at the time must have covered it in detail."

"Both Mr. Prentisse and I were quite aware of that. But his time was limited, and we only keep a back file of *The Times*. I believe he planned to consult the British Library at Colindale eventually; that's where they keep their journals. But his immediate requirement was for an overview of the case."

Miss Winters leaned back in her chair, her lips pursed as if to prevent the escape of secrets. Celia thought of that royal *we* that the librarian used to refer to herself and the library she served: just so would a mother superior refer to her nunnery, and perhaps to God as well. There was also a proprietorial hint in the way Miss Winters mentioned Celia's father: a claiming of kinship that excluded a mere daughter. She wondered if that verdict of suicide was public knowledge here. The *Telegraph* hadn't mentioned it.

"My father often said how much he owed to the London Library." Celia flicked a stray strand of hair away from her glasses. "That you believed in satisfying your customers. Were you able to suggest any other lines of research?"

A faint flush stained Miss Winters's complexion. "As a matter of fact I was. I don't know whether he followed it up, of course. It occurred to me that he could do worse than to consult another of our members: Ruth Guban. You've heard of her?"

"*Jack the Ripper's Other Island*?" suggested William.

"That is probably her best-known book," Miss Winters agreed. "A trifle sensational, but her theory was undoubt-

34

edly ingenious. Many reviewers felt she shouldn't have gilded the lily by arguing that W. B. Yeats was involved as well. Still . . ."

"You've lost me," said Celia with the crispness of irritation. "Ruth Guban writes on crime?"

"Yes. For the general reader, though she's by no means unscholarly. She was at Newnham a little after my time. I believe her work on the Major Armstrong case is considered definitive. And that was arsenic too."

4

THE FLAT WAS in a large, purpose-built Edwardian block at the western end of Fulham Road, not far from Putney Bridge. Ruth Guban lived on the second floor. When she opened the front door to them, a smell of cats and garlic drifted onto the landing. She was a small, stout woman with luxuriantly curly black hair and large brown eyes.

"I don't know why the telephone wouldn't do," she said, "but since you're here I suppose you'd like some tea."

She led the way down the narrow hall, whose walls were covered with dark Victorian engravings. The hall opened into a large living room. A long window, shrouded in half-closed velvet curtains, filled the far wall. In front of it was a table covered with dirty crockery. Ruth Guban stepped over a pile of cat litter whose contents were partly confined to a tray; the rest was on the surrounding carpet, which was fortunately much the same color.

"Do sit down. I'll put the kettle down."

She disappeared into the kitchen, leaving her guests to find room for themselves among the newspapers and books, which covered most of the sofa. William said in an undertone:

36

"Better than she sounds. Wouldn't have offered us tea otherwise."

A large tortoise-shell cat chose this moment to appear from under an armchair and cautiously size them up. He leapt onto William's lap and began to purr, thrusting his head against William's chin in a frenzy of desire for affection.

Celia shifted uneasily on the sofa, automatically taking an inventory of the squalor. Her cleanliness seemed too fragile a barrier for the dirt in this room. William's hand slowly drove the cat to ecstasy.

Ruth Guban returned with the tea tray: three unmatching mugs and a crumpled packet of sugar from which a teaspoon protruded like the sword in the stone. "You don't mind it black," she said firmly. "There's no milk. Or rather there is, but it's so cold that even Ozymandias thinks it's beneath him."

"Am I beneath him now?" William inquired.

"Yes, Mr. . . . I'm sorry, I didn't catch your name."

"Dougal, William Dougal."

Ruth Guban's eyes swung between her two guests. "Just good friends, eh?"

She might have been referring to William and the cat, but Celia doubted it. She passed them their mugs and took her own to the armchair, which had been Ozymandias's refuge.

"One of the drawbacks of my job," she said, "is that people think that since you work at home, you're available at any time. Sometimes I wish I could afford an office."

"My father used to say that too." Celia put down her tea, the surface of which was dotted with an archipelago of gray slime. "We wouldn't have come unless it was important. We'll try not to take up too much of your time."

37

Ruth Guban shrugged. "Doesn't really matter now. I've lost the flow. Anyway, let's get it over with. You said it was in connection with your father's visit the other week. Why couldn't he come himself?"

"I—I thought you'd heard . . ." Celia ran out of words as the memory of her father's absence caught up with her again. Death was like that, it seemed: it retreated from the front of your mind, only to rush out and clobber you when you were least expecting it. Perhaps time would make the blows softer and less frequent. William smoothly scooped up the conversation baton.

"I'm afraid Mr. Prentisse died, a couple of days after seeing you. He was drowned. We're trying to reconstruct the events of his last few days."

"Oh hell, I'm sorry." Ruth Guban covered her embarrassment with a brusque epitaph: "He was a fine historian." Her eyes narrowed; Celia could sense her weighing and testing William's words. She set her mug on the carpet. Ozymandias jumped down to investigate: he sniffed at its contents, sat down with his back to the mug and began to wash his face. "Not an accident?" his mistress said slowly. "Is that what you're implying?"

"There were indications that it was suicide," William said delicately. "But no one has been able to come up with a convincing reason for it. It wasn't in character. So Celia and I—he was my godfather, by the way—are trying to tidy up the loose ends."

"You're sure it was suicide?"

"That's what the coroner said. We wondered if it could be something to do with his work. He had told no one that he was working on the Landis case."

Ruth Guban looked shrewdly at him, as if she was quite aware of the way he had sidestepped her question. "I wish that Winters woman would stop giving out my name to all and sundry."

"What did my father want to know? What did you tell him?"

"As much as I could tell him about the case. Very little is available in print, apart from contemporary sources. Owen's worse than useless—half his facts are inaccurate and he's more concerned with peddling salacious fiction than with telling the truth. I did some research on the case a few years ago; I thought it might be worth including in a collection I was doing on murder for gain. I didn't use it in the end: there wasn't really enough material, and in any case it was too reminiscent of the Seddon case. It was rather a dull little murder."

"But it might be relevant," William suggested. Celia wanted to kick him for the smile he gave Ruth Guban. "Could you tell us what you told Mr. Prentisse?"

Their hostess shrugged. "All right. But I doubt if it will help you. It was basically a family squabble over money, like so many murders."

She left the room for a moment and returned with a brown file. She sat down again and flicked through its contents. As far as Celia could see, there were only a few sheets of handwritten foolscap. Ruth put them down on her lap and started to talk with the impersonality of a lecturer.

The story was not pleasant, and she told it with a certain amount of professional relish. It began with the three Hinton sisters, the daughters of a prosperous bank manager who died a few years before the Great War. Muriel Hinton, the eldest, remained a spinster, a shrewish and domineering woman whose temperament may have owed something to persistent ill health. She was considerably older than her sisters—she was separated from them in the family pecking order by two boys, both of whom died in the war. The middle sister, Alexandra, was thought to have married beneath her—her husband was a village schoolmaster with Socialist leanings. Muriel orchestrated the family disapproval, which increased as Alexandra's income was siphoned off into a variety of worthy causes. Her husband, Alfred Corner, was killed in the war as well. A son was born posthumously, but Alexandra died almost immediately afterward in the great influenza epidemic of 1919.

Muriel made herself responsible for her young nephew. Over the next ten years they lived together in a number of resorts on the south coast. Muriel was a restless woman and rarely settled anywhere for long.

Meanwhile Beatrice, the younger sister, was living with their widowed mother in Barnes. She was a secretary who worked for the Director of a Mayfair motor showroom. In 1929, at the age of twenty-four, she married one of the salesmen. John Landis was ten years older than her. He was an ambitious man who had been commissioned from the ranks during the war; the subsequent decade of civilian life had proved a series of disappointments.

His wife's money provided the couple with a measure of financial security. Landis left the showroom and set up on his own as a motor distributor. They moved to Cambridgeshire and rented a house in a Fen village near Ely. It was not the best time to start up in business, and Landis soon found himself in difficulties. The birth of a son in 1931 increased their expenses. Muriel and their nephew came to live with them as paying guests. The arrangement worked well, despite the occasional squabbles between the sisters; Muriel was nearly twenty years older than Beatrice and was used to ruling the roost. Landis, however, went out of his way to cultivate her.

Muriel had always been subject to gastric attacks and these became more frequent and more severe during the winter of 1931 to 1932. The local doctor visited the house several times, but his prescriptions—chiefly for effervescing mixtures, bismuth, and morphia—failed to effect much material improvement on his patient's health. After a prolonged and particularly savage attack at the end of February, Muriel died in her sleep. The doctor, who had last seen her thirty-six hours earlier, made out a death certificate; the cause of death was given as epidemic diarrhea. Muriel was buried a few days later.

But for two circumstances she might have remained undisturbed. Her will left her entire estate to her sister and brother-in-law, with Landis as the executor. Old Mrs. Hinton, whose character was not dissimilar to that of her eldest daughter, was enraged. She demanded the return of certain pieces of jewelry, which, she claimed, had only been lent to her daughter. Mr. Landis appeared unable to find them. This developed into a bitter dispute about Muriel's money.

Fate played into Mrs. Hinton's hands when the doctor was arrested. Apart from his normal practice he had a flourishing sideline in back-street abortions in Cambridge. Doubt about his professional integrity tipped the balance. Muriel's body was exhumed and found to contain several grains of arsenic.

Mr. and Mrs. Landis were arrested and charged with the murder. Both asserted their innocence: each put the blame on the other. Circumstantial evidence mounted up. Landis's business was ailing. He had persuaded

Muriel to make over to him four small houses in Richmond and a number of stocks and shares, in return for an annuity. He admitted that he had sold most of her jewelry. The Crown was able to prove that some pieces, including a diamond necklace that Mrs. Hinton claimed was hers, had been sold in the January before Muriel's death. Doubt was cast on the validity of the will: Muriel's signature was shakier than usual—Landis explained that she had been ill at the time.

A half-used packet of arsenic was found in the garden shed. Landis said that he had bought this the previous October to deal with rats which were coming across from a nearby farm. Both the maid and the jobbing gardener confirmed this, though the latter was certain that only a quarter of the packet had been used.

Landis could not remember where he had bought the poison. The purchase was not recorded at any local chemist's shop. It was unfortunate for Landis that his photograph appeared in the papers: a pharmacist in Brewer Street, Soho, recognized his face. The prosecution was given an unexpected bonus when it was discovered that he had signed the poisons register with the name of John Evans. Landis explained this by claiming that he had spent the day and the following night with a prostitute, whom he knew only as Lil; he had given a false name because she was with him at the chemist's, and he didn't want her to learn his real identity.

His defense was undermined by the fact that the chemist had not noticed his alleged companion; it was destroyed when subsequent enquiries failed to bring forward the Soho prostitute. The affair served to establish that Landis habitually mixed business with pleasure on his travels, which did nothing to recommend him to the twelve Cambridge shopkeepers and Fen farmers on the jury. The counsel for the defense argued that Landis's initial reluctance to remember where he had bought the arsenic was due to an admirable desire to spare his wife knowledge of his extramarital activities. Most people, however, took it as a clear indication that the murder had been premeditated for some time.

Traces of arsenic were found in a decanter of brandy in Miss Hinton's bedroom. A police search of the house also uncovered a small quantity of the poison in an envelope, which had been squeezed down between the seat and the arm of the chair in John Landis's study. The evidence of the little maid showed that Landis had been unusually concerned about his sister-in-law's illness. Sometimes he prepared drinks for her—chiefly brandy and hot water, meat extract and tea—and often took them up to her himself. Two days before she died, when she had a particularly bad attack, he canceled all his business appointments in order to stay at home and help nurse her.

Landis pleaded not guilty during his trial, but the weight of evidence was against him. Mrs. Landis was acquitted—there was nothing to show that she was aware of her husband's precarious financial position, or even of the presence of arsenic in the garden shed. John Landis, however, was executed in September 1932.

Ruth Guban pushed the notes into the file and tossed it on the floor beside her chair. "That's it, I'm afraid. Unlike Seddon, no one seriously suggested that Landis was innocent, either then or later. He continued to blame his wife for the murder right up to his death."

"But why was my father interested? It was completely outside his usual field."

Ruth shrugged. "He didn't confide in me. Said it would

be premature. I gained the impression that he'd stumbled across something which could throw new light on it. But he wasn't sure enough to commit himself."

"Afraid of going off at half-cock?"

"Something like that. He said he'd let me know if he did discover there was a book in it."

William leant forward. "We found a note in his diary. It looked like *med to mum 481*. Does that mean anything to you?"

Ruth shook her head. "It wasn't mentioned. I suppose the *mum* could be Beatrice. Or maybe Mrs. Hinton. But it doesn't really make sense." She ran her fingers through her curls. "He did ask about the survivors, though. Presumably he was thinking of tracing them. It wouldn't have been an easy course—it was over fifty years ago, and people mixed up in murder cases often change their names afterwards. It's just possible that Beatrice might still be alive. She was much younger than Muriel and her husband."

"And the maid," suggested William.

"Don't forget the children," Celia said. "The son and the orphaned nephew. You've no idea what happened to them?"

Ruth gave a short bark of laughter, which lacked any trace of amusement. "God knows. I often wonder what happens to the bystanders. The innocent friends and relatives. And the kids—especially the kids. It must be like having an earthquake in your life. When the tremors die down you must still feel you're living on top of a seismic fault. Liable to erupt at any moment. Maybe you get over it eventually."

"Not necessarily." William looked rather white; Celia thought it might be due to the fading light. "Violent

44

death doesn't have a place in most people's lives. But when it does, you . . . you must feel the possibility of it is always there. I don't think you'd ever get away from that."

5

As MAJOR DOUGAL stood in front of the bathroom mirror on Sunday morning, an idea occurred to him. For a moment he stared at his face—one half pink, smooth, and faintly shiny, the other as uniformly white as Antarctica—and tried to decide whether the idea was anything more than a con trick that one half of his mind was playing on the other. If that were so, the purpose of the idea was purely therapeutic: to make him feel that there was more to being an old-age pensioner than waiting on the sidelines of life until death touched one's shoulder.

He pulled tight the skin of his neck and drove a crisp swath of pink up to his jawline. The blade of the razor sliced into a fold of skin. A line of red spread across the surface of the cut. He reached for the cotton wool and made up his mind to go to church.

There was no point in asking William if he wanted to come, on the same principle that one doesn't ask publicans for credit: a refusal can only offend. Besides, the boy was asleep. He had taken Celia out to dinner last night and hadn't returned until two in the morning. Major Dougal knew because he had lain awake, waiting and worrying, until he heard William's key in the front door. Old habits die hard, even when you want nothing better than to see them dead.

He breakfasted at nine on a solitary boiled egg. The yolk was runny; so, unfortunately, was the white. He spooned the two colors into a streaky mixture, stabbed at it with a finger of toast and pulled William's notes toward him.

He had read them last night—William had dropped in with them in the early evening. They outlined the conversation with Ruth Guban with admirable concision. The boy might have made a good staff officer. But the information in the notes did nothing to shake the Major's faith in the coroner's verdict. It was true that Richard Prentisse had acted out of character—both in attempting to exhume an old murder and in killing himself. But the facts on which the verdict was based remained. Moreover, it was foolish to expect a person to act according to a pattern of behavior you deduced from his past actions. Take William, for example: Who would have expected that episode ten years ago?

It was a fine morning, though with enough of autumn in the air to make a brisk walking pace necessary. Major Dougal, swinging an umbrella as insurance, strode smartly down the hill to St. Clement's at the end of Market Street. The service, a family communion presided over by the bearded curate, was just about to begin when he arrived on the dot of nine-thirty. The Major thought the atmosphere resembled a crèche rather than a church. He slid into his usual pew, and nodded to the two Misses Baines who were surreptitiously sucking the first Murray Mints of the service. He opened his hymnal and let his eyes stray down the church in search of his quarry.

Celia and Margaret were on the other side of the nave, considerably closer to the choir than he was. They were a little apart, as if their bodies had automatically left room for Richard.

The service slowly moved to its close while babies wailed and their elder brothers and sisters scampered up and down the aisles. Major Dougal planned his tactics with precision. He was one of the first out of the church.

"Morning, Ted," said the curate, who was already lying in wait for his flock in the porch. "I thought we'd get you to the family service sooner or later. Rather wonderful to have the kids around. Suffer the little children, and so forth."

"Hmm. Lovely morning." Major Dougal scuttled past into the open air. He privately thought that the word *suffer* was remarkably apt. He stood blinking in the sunlight, absently digging the tip of his umbrella into the grass at his feet.

Margaret and Celia emerged shortly afterwards in company with Mrs. Grimes and the two Misses Baines. The packet of Murray Mints was now in the open. The curate declined one. Celia stopped beside Major Dougal with a smile. The elder Miss Baines continued to talk to her, the bulge in her left cheek bobbing up and down.

"Are you sure you won't come, dear? Do you good to get away for a few hours."

"No, I really mustn't," Celia said quickly. "I arranged to meet someone for lunch in any case."

The presence of the Major prevented the older women from asking the obvious question.

Celia turned to him with a rapidity that suggested he was a welcome diversion. "Uncle Ted, Margaret and I were wondering if you'd like any of Daddy's books. Most of them are going to be sold, and I know he'd have liked you to have first option."

"Yes, do take a few if you want to, Ted," said Margaret with a marked lack of enthusiasm. "Every little bit helps.

48

There's so much stuff in that house I sometimes feel it's oozing out of the walls at me."

Mrs. Grimes and the two Misses Baines cooed in a sympathetic chorus.

"Very kind of you, Margaret." The Major stared at the tip of his umbrella.

"You can come up to the house now if you want to," Celia suggested.

"By all means," said Margaret Prentisse, regaining the initiative. "Unfortunately, I can't come with you—Norah and I are going to Jenny's and Betty's for lunch. But I'm sure Celia will look after you. As far as her own social engagements permit."

Miaow, thought Major Dougal.

The party split up at the lych gate. Major Dougal offered Celia his arm.

"Thanks," Celia said after they had gone a few yards. "I could have got out of the lunch but without you it would've been hard to avoid a dose of the preliminary sherry and scandal. They can't wait to find out all about it."

"Which 'it' have they got in mind?"

"Me and William. They know we spent most of yesterday together. Margaret even knows what time I got back last night because she stayed awake. And now they're pretty sure I'll be seeing him at lunchtime."

"I suppose I'm a little curious too." Major Dougal tried not to think of how he had stayed awake last night.

"You're different. As a matter of fact, we were going to drive to Little Champney. There's a pub there that does sausages and garlic bread; and the beer is pretty good too. We both wanted to ask you to come."

"You don't have to say that."

49

"Well, it's true. There's nothing private between me and William. I've been living with Jim for two years, remember? We're going to get married. Once he gets his deputy headship." She raised her free hand as if to prove her point. The diamond on her ring finger twinkled in the sunlight.

The Major had met Jim. He was five years older than Celia, and a colleague at the comprehensive where she taught. He was a sober-minded ambitious individual with a broken nose and a rugger player's body running to seed. Richard had thought his future son-in-law a bore, but that was neither here nor there.

"I just don't want you to get hurt again," he said hesitantly. "It's not that I don't think you're capable of looking after yourself. It's just that I don't altogether trust my own son."

Celia stopped abruptly, her fingers digging into his arm. "That's not *fair*, Uncle Ted. Like Daddy and everyone else around here, you judged him; but you didn't bother to find out the whole story."

"Didn't bother? Didn't need to. The facts spoke for themselves. There were ninety-eight pounds in that cashbox in my bureau, the proceeds from that damned jumble sale, waiting to be banked on the Monday. He knew the money was there and he stole it, just so he could take a schoolgirl away for an impressively lavish weekend. I know you weren't aware of how he'd got the money at the time and I'm not blaming you for any of it. He behaved in a thoroughly shabby way and that's all there is to say about it."

Major Dougal started walking; he inadvertently tugged Celia, who was still attached to his arm, causing her to stumble. "Sorry, my dear," he said, and jabbed his umbrella at the unyielding pavement.

50

"He . . . he paid the money back, didn't he?"

"That's not the point. Yes, he did. With interest and a little note of apology perhaps a couple of months afterward. But it was too late. I knew what had happened and so did Mrs. Gann. That was in the days when she worked for me as well. So that meant the whole of Plumford knew."

They walked on in silence. Celia's words had undammed an inexorable tide of bitter memories. The theft had been all the more shocking because it had happened at a time when Major Dougal had hopes that his son was at last going to grow up and settle down. He had been in his last year at Cambridge, talking of going on to do research and showing a seemingly responsible interest in Celia. Then he had wantonly hurt the very people who were closest to him. It had taken Celia months, if not years, to recover from the business. As for himself—

"Uncle Ted. It was my fault."

"Don't be ridiculous. He's four years older than you and he knew exactly what he was doing."

Celia began to walk faster. "About ten weeks before that weekend, he took me to a party. We had a quarrel, because I thought this other girl fancied him and he was encouraging it." She spoke softly and monotonously as if reciting a dull and familiar lesson. "I got horribly drunk and ended up losing my virginity to the birthday boy whose party it was. Then I was sick and went to have a good cry in the garden. William eventually found me there. He cleaned me up, calmed me down and took me home. A month later I realized I was pregnant. Two months later I managed to find the courage to tell him. Neither of us had any money. And I couldn't tell my parents. Or you. William said not to worry. He fixed up everything. He took me to his doctor in Cambridge.

51

Booked me in at a private clinic. Refused to tell me how he'd got the money. Insisted that I had a room with color TV and fresh flowers. He slept in a friend's van outside the clinic. There you are, Uncle Ted, that's what I did on my dirty weekend: had an abortion."

"You two young idiots." Major Dougal stopped to blow his nose with the vigor of a trumpeter announcing victory. "Why didn't one of you tell me? You could have explained afterward if not at the time."

"We agreed not to. William made me promise. He said you'd feel it was your duty to tell my father. You know how he would have reacted—that stuff about the sanctity of human life didn't just apply to suicide. And he wouldn't have been able to keep it from Margaret, even if he'd wanted to, poor thing."

"But since your father died. . . ?" Major Dougal realized with a shock that William had read him correctly: he would have felt obliged to tell Richard. You don't tell lies, even by omission, to someone who scraped you off a Normandy beach in 1944 at considerable risk to his own safety.

"The situation changed. I told William last night I was going to see you. I wanted to tell you after the funeral, off my own bat. But I couldn't when I found William was there." Her voice suddenly hardened. "Thank God it's over. You've no idea how bloody humiliating it is to bear the burden of someone else's self-sacrifice."

The Major was finding difficulty concentrating. His mind felt as if it had been physically shaken, like a snowstorm beneath a glass dome. He heard himself saying: "Perhaps I will accept your invitation to lunch."

They had arrived at the Prentisses' front gate. Major Dougal held it open for Celia to pass through. The sight of the house reminded him of his original purpose in coming here. He seized upon the memory gratefully, ignoring the snowflakes that danced around it.

"I read the notes William made last night," he said as they climbed the stairs to the study. "They didn't change my mind," he added hastily. "But I had an idea that might be worth putting to the test."

Celia glanced back over her shoulder. "What about?"

"You'll see."

The study smell immediately assailed the Major. Part of it reminded him of Richard. But there was also a new element, a hint of mustiness and disuse, which brought home to him the fact of Richard's death far more vividly than those bizarre rites of passage at the crematorium. He swayed against the door frame, clutching at one of the uprights.

Celia was beside him in an instant, holding his other arm. "Uncle Ted! What is it?"

He shook his head. She guided him to an armchair.

"Would you like some water? Or brandy?"

For a moment he thought he saw her father's face poised anxiously above him. *Forty years ago: another time, another place.*

"No. I'm fine." He was surprised to find it was true. "Don't fuss, there's a dear." Celia backed away, uncertain how she should take the rejection. Major Dougal smiled. "I really am all right. Shall we get on with it?"

"If you're sure . . . ?"

He nodded. "Right. Where's that encyclopedia?"

"You're welcome to have it if you want, but it's amazingly heavy. We'd need the car. Look at it."

She pointed toward the three columns of dark blue volumes, which reared like a forgotten Stonehenge of knowl-

53

edge in the corner. Major Dougal got stiffly to his feet and crossed the room toward them. He picked up the nearest volume. It measured about twelve by eight by three inches; its weight surprised him. A black pattern had faded into near invisibility on the cover. He looked closer and recognized the arms of the Cambridge University Press. He turned the book so he could see the gold lettering on the spine: Volume Two.

"William used that on Friday," Celia said. She sucked in her breath as if she had stubbed her toe. "He looked up arsenic."

Major Dougal returned Volume Two to its pile, cocked his head on one side and ran his eyes down each of the columns in turn.

"Ah," he said quietly. "Here we are." With a jerk he pulled out the second volume from the top in the center pile. A cloud of dust momentarily blurred the outline of his hands. "Volume Eighteen." He disliked the smugness he could hear creeping into his own voice. "MED TO MUM."

6

"CORNER!" SAID MAJOR DOUGAL, with a broad smile across his face and a forgotten section of French bread oozing garlic butter onto his hand. "Corner is the key to all this." It was difficult to avoid a touch of euphoria when you had but recently discovered that you were neither as solitary nor as useless as you had feared. He sat back, swallowed a quarter of a pint of Abbot's Ale and wiped his mouth.

William spread a piece of sausage with his fork. "Would one of you mind telling me what the excitement's about? I feel left out."

Celia, who was also grinning idiotically, said: "Your father's worked out the *med to mum* problem. And leading on from that we may have found the reason why Daddy was straying outside his usual area of research. Or seeming to."

"I had a hunch, you see." The Major coughed apologetically, as if intuition was a faculty he preferred not to acknowledge in public. "I wondered if the *med to mum* could be a reference to a multi-volumed book. Not many around with that number of volumes. Then I remembered that encyclopedia Richard bought."

"He wouldn't tell me beforehand," said Celia."Had to have his little surprise."

55

"Well, yes. One would have felt so stupid if one was wrong."

"But one wasn't?" asked William dryly.

"The lettering on the spine fitted precisely. Page 481 was in the middle of the article about Milton. Never had much time for him as a poet. A bit too self-righteous for his own good."

"What was *there?*"

"Nothing. Absolutely nothing. But there had been. You could see a slight indentation, about ten by eight inches, on both pages. The paper had got discolored—damp, I suppose—so there was a faint trace of brown at three of the corners."

"So you're assuming Uncle Richard found a bit of paper tucked away in there?"

"It seems likely. He must have found something, or else he wouldn't have made the note in his diary." Major Dougal paused to finish off his pint. "We tried all the other volumes, just in case."

"There were twenty-nine," Celia interrupted. "Our hands got filthy."

"But all we found were a couple of bookmarks in the index volume, just inside the front cover. Quite old—maybe nineteen-thirties—but no distinguishing marks on them. My guess is that Richard put them there. If he stumbled on whatever Milton contained he'd be sure to check the rest."

"Okay," William said slowly. "I can accept that. But how do you make a link with the Landis case?" His eyes widened in surprise as Celia giggled.

"I'm sorry," she said. "It turned out to be so obvious. The original owner had put his name on the flyleaf of each volume: A. X. Corner."

"Corner . . . the name of the brother-in-law who was

killed in the Great War? The schoolmaster who wasn't good enough for the Hinton family?"

"Absolutely." Major Dougal gathered up the three empty glasses with an emphatic clink. "We've established a clear chain, I think: Richard buys the *Britannica*; his curiosity is ignited by whatever he finds on page 481 of Volume Eighteen; his preliminary researches would have been helped by the flyleaf—Corner isn't a common name, after all; and so he starts investigating the Landis case."

"But—" William began.

"Just a moment." Major Dougal moved away toward the bar, disappearing into a knot of Sunday lunchtime drinkers and their dogs. It was fortunate, he reflected, that they had got that table in the bay window. It was an island of privacy protected by the barrier reefs of loud, self-absorbed conversation. More and more people with booming voices, large dogs, and glossy Wellington boots were buying weekend cottages around Plumford. It was a tribute to the Divine Plan that even these immigrants could have their uses.

His faith in the efficacy of the Divine Plan was somewhat shaken by the length of time it took him to get served. Surely by his age he should have learned the knack of catching the barman's eye? At length he was able to buy three more pints. Celia's desire to drink like a man worried him as much as her apparent ability to do so.

He managed to return to their table without spilling much of the beer on the way. William smiled as he set the drinks down. Major Dougal realized that in his absence Celia would have been telling William about their conversation after church. He felt dangerously happy.

"Now, father," William said—in an almost proprietorial voice, surely?—"perhaps you'd like to enlighten me further. It's obvious you two are sitting on something else." He lit a cigarette and made a half-hearted attempt to keep the smoke away from Celia's face.

"You remember Richard kept a card index?"

William nodded. "In one of the gray filing cabinets. There must be about a million five-by-three cards there."

"He was very proud of it," the Major continued. "Used to boast about it, actually. He started it just after the war when he was doing his first book. It's a simple alphabetical sequence of names and places and so forth. He claimed that because his books generally covered the same period, the index allowed him to make countless connections he would never otherwise have made. Cumulatively so."

"He had a joke about that," Celia said softly. "Ultimately the index was going to make him nearly superfluous. He would just feed in an idea, a name or something, and the index would make all the connections. He'd have to look up the references and type it all out. Or rather I would—I've been doing most of the secretarial work in the last couple of years."

"A sort of historian's Frankenstein?" William suggested. "He should have got a computer. What did you find?"

Major Dougal began to stack their dirty plates. "Nothing under Landis or Hinton. But we struck gold with Corner, Alfred X. It must be the same man, given that second initial. Xavier, I imagine."

William sighed. "But all that confirms is that Uncle Richard was seriously looking into the case. Which we knew already."

"Rather more than that." The Major's eyes gleamed

58

beneath the white spikes of his eyebrows. "The card held three bits of information." He held up his left hand and with his right ticked off a finger for each item. "One: 'Died 1918'—which supports our identification of this Corner with ours. Two: 'See Snowden'; I'll come back to that. Richard was a methodical sort of chap, which brings us to three: he noted the date when he made out the card. Not last month. It was almost three years ago."

"In other words—" William began slowly.

Celia broke in: "We've found Daddy's line of approach. It solves the problem of why he was concerned with something outside his usual field. Maybe the Landis case was mentioned in whatever was in *med to mum*. But Corner's named linked it to one of his existing interests."

"Three years ago," William said as he stubbed out his cigarette, "your father must have been working on *Military Men*. Did he get the title from Talleyrand? War is much too serious a thing to be left to military men."

"And much too dangerous to be entrusted to damn-fool civilians," said Major Dougal.

"How did you know?" Celia said simultaneously. She knew she was indulging in a digression; but she found it oddly comforting to think of the unknown William of the last ten years reading her father's books.

"I bought it when it came out. It dealt with the army's relationship with the general public. If I remember right, it carried on to the end of the Great War, didn't it?"

Celia nodded. "That's where Philip Snowden came in. He was the leader of a group of Labor MPs who wanted Britain out of the war. The government and the army found him uncomfortably well informed, especially when it came to particular instances of injustice. Daddy thought he was helped by sympathizers in the army and

59

the civil service. According to his rough notes for the book, there was a possibility that Corner was one of them. But he couldn't prove it."

"Not a bad chap, Snowden," said the Major unexpectedly. "I know he was a pacifist or next best thing to it, but at least he *cared* about the men in the trenches. A lot of MPs didn't want to know."

William remarked to his glass of beer: "I suppose you've sorted out how this ties in with Uncle Richard's death?"

There was silence around the table. Major Dougal scratched his head. He could feel the tranquility of the last half hour oozing away, like sand from an hourglass. Still, it was better to have had it, if only for a short time.

"Ah," he said cautiously. "That's another matter." He glanced surreptitiously at Celia. He felt as if he were walking with muddy shoes across a newly polished floor. But there was no alternative. "I've not changed my mind. We've solved a minor mystery: why Richard was looking into something that was outside his usual beat. But nothing we've discovered qualifies the coroner's findings." He put his brown-spotted hand on Celia's. "I'm sorry, my dear, but there it is. The facts remain."

Celia snatched her hand away. "Like the bottle of gin and all the other discrepancies."

"There's not a lot more we can do." As Major Dougal knew from his own experience, it could be dangerous to become obsessed with the past; in particular, a death could haunt you. He tried to switch Celia's attention from the ghosts in her mind: "Besides, you're due back to school tomorrow. If I were you, I'd try a week or two of normal life, and then sit back and reassess the situation. Talk it over with Jim. An outside opinion could be useful. Perhaps William and I are too closely involved."

Celia took a deep breath and gently laid her hand on Major Dougal's. "I rang Jim after breakfast this morning. I told him I was taking at least another week's compassionate leave. He didn't like it, but he'll have to lump it. I can't help it if he thinks CSE English and the end-of-term concert are more important than my father's death. I'm sorry, Uncle Ted, but sod him. And sod you too if you agree with him."

William intervened with a tactful clearing of his throat. Celia rounded on him.

"And don't you patronize me either. We're not a pair of kids any more." Celia got to her feet and picked up the car keys. "I'm going home now. Do you two want a lift?"

William stared up at her, his face giving no indication of his feelings. Major Dougal wondered with sudden panic how on earth he was going to bridge that decade of mutual ignorance, which separated him from his son.

"I have a suggestion," William said. "Do you know, there's one possibility we haven't even thought of exploring."

7

CELIA JUMPED AS the bell above their heads jangled like a jarred nerve. Some shop bells merely announce your arrival; others make the announcement into a warning. *Look out!* this one seemed to be saying, *the people entering this establishment are potential shoplifters with past records of child rape and armed robbery.*

She preceded William into the small, square front room of the shop. The rear wall had been knocked down, extending the shop into what had been once the back parlor when this was a private house. Shelves of unvarnished pine ran around the walls. They had clearly been erected without the benefit of a spirit level. In the center of the room was a cluster of free-standing wire racks, filled with faded paperbacks. Beside them was a battered card table laden with hardbacks. *20p each* said a placard pinned to the back of the table. A desperate footnote had been added, perhaps at a later date: *Or 7 for £1.* The contents of both the table and the racks were splotched with rain. She and William had been caught out by the rain this morning too.

They were the only people in the shop. There was no one behind the desk at the back. William pulled out a volume on Suffolk churches from a shelf marked LOCAL

62

INTEREST. He thumbed it open, glanced at the flyleaf and the title page and slid it back on the shelf. He looked at the dust on his fingers with an expression of disgust on his face. The impression of fastidiousness was spoiled when he wiped his hands on his trousers.

"Overpriced," he said. "I don't suppose there's much demand for local interest in Champney Crucis."

"Perhaps most of the trade is by mail," Celia suggested charitably. Like William, she kept her voice down. Perhaps the bell was listening. "The shop's only been open a few months."

William wandered across to the card table. Celia's eyes followed him. When she had arrived to collect him this morning he had surprised her by appearing in a suit— gray, with a faint pinstripe. The collar of his white shirt stood out vividly against his tanned neck. Smartness was not a quality she associated with William. This unexpected formal elegance seemed exotic.

A lavatory flushed somewhere above their heads. A door slammed. There was the sound of heavy shoes clattering down an uncarpeted staircase. This was followed by a stumble, a confused series of thuds, and the words "Oh bother!" spoken in a deep, booming voice.

A door behind and to the right of the desk burst open. An immensely tall man shot into the shop. The desk brought him to a stop in the same way that buffers halt a runaway train.

William and Celia stared up at him. He was closer to seven feet than six feet in height, or would have been if his neck had not been bent forwards in what was probably an habitual forty-five degree angle from the perpendicular. His head was surmounted by a shock of gray, wiry hair. He was wearing a collarless blue shirt, which looked as if it had come from a charity shop, and filthy jeans. The shirt sleeves were rolled above the elbow. His long, bony arms dangled down to the desk. They ended in a pair of massive hands, curled into fists and sprinkled with clumps of black hair.

He raised his face by a fraction, revealing large, dark brown eyes, cadaverous cheeks, and a long, broken nose, which had reset itself out of true.

"May I be of any assistance?" he inquired. "Or are you just browsing?" His voice carried around the little shop, bouncing off the walls and blurring like the roar of Atlantic surf.

"We have some questions," William said. He moved toward the desk. Celia glanced at him: his voice sounded different—it was harder and flatter than usual, almost foxy. She noticed that he had a couple of paperbacks in one hand.

"From the rack?" said the man behind the desk. "Twenty pence each."

William laid a pound note on the blotter between them. "According to our information," he said pompously, "you are the proprietor of this shop. Your name, please?"

"Chanter. Joshua Chanter." The tip of Mr. Chanter's nose gave a disconcerting twitch. "What is this? Who are you?"

William's lips tightened. He fished inside his jacket, produced his wallet, extracted a card and flashed it across the desk. Celia caught a glimpse of plastic lamination and a color photograph.

"Detective Sergeant Bowen." William jerked a thumb toward Celia. "And DC Jones." With a flourish he returned the wallet to his pocket. "We won't take up much of your time, sir. I hope not."

Mr. Chanter blinked twice. "The Boreham Hall sale," he said unhappily. "I explained to Mr. Carter at the time. It was a genuine mistake. There were two tea chests, you see. Someone on the auctioneer's staff had chalked Carter on one and Chanter on the other. I misread it, that's all. There was no need for him to get so unpleasant in the car park."

"I doubt if Mr. Carter will bring charges," said William with oracular finality. "No, sir, it's another matter. Do you remember selling a set of the *Encyclopedia Britannica* last August?"

"The eleventh edition," Mr. Chanter said with some excitement. "1910, but still the best for the humanities."

He was trembling slightly. Like many people, he was sent slightly off balance by the presence of the police. Celia tried not to look at his hands, which were palpitating like a pair of agitated tarantulas.

"We know that, sir, and that you sold it to a Mr. Prentisse—"

"Seventy-five pounds," thundered Mr. Chanter. "A bargain. The set was in excellent condition. I could have got more if I'd been prepared to wait. But it was a matter of cash flow. Naturally I recorded the full details of the transaction—"

"Mr. Chanter," William interrupted, "we know what happened to the set. Our concern is with its provenance. Where did you get it?"

"In an auction. It was the Boreham Hall sale, in fact. That was in July."

"Was it a book sale?"

"No." Mr. Chanter disclaimed the idea with his arm, in a gesture that propelled a bottle of ink from the desk to the floor. The top was evidently loose: a black glistening puddle spread around the bottle and was quickly ab-

65

sorbed by the light blue carpet. "Oh *no.*" Mr. Chanter dropped to his knees and stooped over the bottle. He extended his forefinger and gingerly touched the black patch. "It's only a few months old. The carpet, I mean."

Celia knelt down, taking a wad of tissues from her handbag. She righted the bottle, recapped it and placed in on the table. "It would be black, wouldn't it?"

"It gets everywhere." Mr. Chanter struggled back to his feet and stared helplessly at his blackened fingers. He wiped them on his jeans. "Like glue. Anything you do just seems to make it worse."

"Try salt," Celia suggested. "Soak up as much as you can and then wash it in warm, sudsy water. If that fails, you'll have to try some sort of bleach. But that might affect the blue."

"*I* know." Mr. Chanter beamed. "If we move the desk two feet that way"—Mr. Chanter gestured again; Celia caught the pile of books before it fell—"it'll cover the stain."

"The Boreham Hall sale," said William harshly. "Was it just for books?"

"No, no." Mr. Chanter shook his head violently. "House clearance. Quite a small one. I thought with a name like that the house would be pretty big, but in fact it's just a glorified Victorian house. Perhaps I'd better go and wash."

"Just a minute. Do you know who lived at the house?"

"I think it was a couple of old ladies. One had died and the other was selling up. But I could be wrong. I probably am."

"Their names?" demanded William. "Where is Boreham Hall in any case?"

"Sorry, sergeant, I don't think anyone mentioned who

66

they were. But Boreham's a few miles south of Stowmarket. Near Luggenhall. Now, if you'll excuse me . . ."

"One more thing." William tapped the pound note on the desk. "My change."

"Did you have to be so unpleasant to that poor man?" asked Celia.

They were sitting in the Deux Chevaux. It had begun to rain far harder just before they left the shop. The fifty-yard dash to the car had left them both dripping.

William shrugged. "It was the easiest way to get what we wanted out of him. I didn't plan it like that."

"You never used to be so nasty. You've changed."

"We both have," said William gently. "It's been ten years, remember?"

"And why did you pretend to be a cop? It's a criminal offense. What if Chanter checks up? Do you always carry a fake warrant card?"

"Chanter won't check. Why should he? As for the card, it's an expired reader's ticket to the British Museum Reading Room. I showed it to him upside down for two seconds. Do you mind if I smoke?"

"Yes!" said Celia. "I bloody well do."

William opened the window and lit a cigarette. They glared at one another. Then William laughed.

"I'm sorry," he said. "Pretending to be a policeman made me lose my sense of proportion." He inhaled again and flicked the cigarette out of the window.

His hand dropped onto her shoulder. *The fraternal touch*, thought Celia bitterly. She leaned forward to start the engine, a maneuver designed to force William to remove his hand.

He didn't.

The engine fired. Celia put her hand on William's, gave it a brief squeeze and lifted it off.

"I'm not a teenager any more." She knew she sounded prim; she wished she felt it was true.

William grinned. "Nor am I, thank God. Shall we try Boreham now?"

"I suppose so." She put the car into gear and executed a messy four-point turn. "But no more policemen, okay?"

"Okay. It seems to bring out the worst in me."

They drove in silence for a couple of miles. Their route took them away from Plumford.

"I've thought of something," Celia said. "We should ring your father and let him know what we're doing. And we can ask him what he thought of that letter."

They found a telephone box in the center of the village outside the post office. Celia parked on the double yellow lines beside it. William ran through the rain to the kiosk while she sat in the car, her fingers picking at the steering-wheel cover. William was back sooner than she had expected. He plunged into the car with a slight frown on his face.

"That's odd. There was no answer. He was only going to the corner shop, so he should have been home by now."

8

MAJOR DOUGAL RETURNED from the corner shop just before it started to rain. He knew at once that the bungalow was empty—he had had plenty of practice at recognizing the symptoms. He fancied it was something to do with the increased resonance of the noises he made. Celia must have come a little earlier than planned.

He went to the kitchen to make a cup of tea with a tea bag. He was pleased to see that William had done the breakfast washing-up. He took the tea into the sitting room, collecting the newspaper from the hall table on the way. As he entered, his eyes automatically strayed toward his wife's photograph.

A large white envelope was propped up on the shelf just to the right of the photograph. The Major could see the words UNCLE TED on it even at this distance. He put down the tea and the paper, turned on the gas fire and picked up the envelope. Underneath his name Celia had scribbled: *Found the enclosed in Daddy's correspondence file for* Military Men. *Any ideas?*

With the envelope in his hand, Major Dougal sat down and sipped his tea. He felt an almost superstitious dread about opening it. He turned it over and saw that it was unsealed. Inside was a fragment of the past. The present was bad enough without wantonly complicating life still further by bringing up what was dead and gone.

He shook the contents of the envelope on to his lap. There were three sheets of paper, held together by a rusting paper clip. On top was a page torn from a short-hand pad, containing a few words in Richard Prentisse's neat hand. *CORNER: rang PRO (x2412). Referred to M.o.D.–Grainger.* Beneath this was a blurred carbon copy of a letter, addressed to Mr. Grainger at the Ministry of Defense.

Richard explained that he wanted to consult the file of Lieutenant Alfred Xavier Corner, died 1918, for the purposes of historical research; the Public Records Office had referred him to Mr. Grainger.

The bottom sheet of paper was Grainger's reply. It was dated nearly a month after Prentisse's letter and was terse to the point of rudeness. The file on Lieutenant Corner had not been released to the PRO and was unlikely to be in the foreseeable future.

Major Dougal folded the pieces of paper and restored them to their envelope. Richard had come up against a blank wall: Corner was a cul-de-sac, and that was that. He flicked the envelope on to the sofa. It landed face up against the arm. UNCLE TED, it said reproachfully, UNCLE TED.

The Major finished his tea and tried to become absorbed in the newspaper. Despite himself, he found his eyes wandering across the room toward the sofa. He let the newspaper slip out of his hands.

It was a blank wall, all right, built of indestructible bureaucratic bricks and probably cemented by the Official Secrets Act. But there would be chinks—there always were if you knew where to look for them and had the right tools to exploit them.

In the final analysis the decision rested with himself. The road to Corner, if followed, had to take him through his own past. If he followed it, the Major reckoned that he had a slightly better than even chance of reaching his destination. But there would be dragons on the way; and the dragons in that part of the world had a habit of exacting tolls on your journey. He had assiduously avoided the dragons for the last few years. Why did he have to change his policy now?

UNCLE TED, UNCLE TED.

Major Dougal levered himself out of the chair and stalked into the hall. He pounced on the telephone as if it was the neck of a particularly obnoxious dragon. His finger dialed the familiar number of its own accord. His mind shot off on a tangent, calculating the cost of a call to London at the peak morning rate.

The telephone was answered after three rings. There was the usual burst of static, followed by "—Can I help you?" in a bored female voice.

"Colonel Blaines, please. My name's Frederick Forester."

A pause. A click. Then the woman's voice returned. "I'm sorry, sir. We have no one of that name listed here. If you leave your number, I'll—"

"My mistake," interruped the Major. "I misdialed the second digit. Sorry to trouble you. Good-bye."

He glanced at his watch, returned to the sitting room and gave the newspaper another chance. For the next twelve minutes he read and reread an advertisement for engineers in Saudi Arabia. Then the telephone rang.

He reached it without indecent haste, picked it up and said, "Plumford 3534."

"Ted, me old cock," roared a medium-sized dragon with a heart of steel. "Nice to feel your digit in my pie again."

❖   ❖   ❖

Major Dougal snapped open his umbrella as he emerged from Green Park underground station onto the north side of Piccadilly. He turned right and threaded his way along the crowded pavement. He walked briskly, weaving, accelerating and slowing with the expertise of a minnow in a busy stream. It was surprising how quickly one's urban reflexes returned.

He turned into White Horse Street, a relative backwater where it was possible to move more quickly. He was a few minutes late. Shepherd Market took him by surprise, as it always did. Compared with the surrounding streets it was designed on such a small scale. Its alleys were seething with tourists. He turned left by the Bunch of Grapes and in a few seconds was outside Valentino's.

The faded awning still hung drunkenly along the frontage. There were two tables outside, both with little puddles of water in their ashtrays. Major Dougal furled his umbrella and stepped into the warm gloom of the restaurant.

The room was thick with smoke and with the smells of cooking. It was as he remembered it—the cramped tables crowded with gobbling eaters, the middle-aged English waitresses, and the taciturn cockney-Italian proprietor presiding over the cash register behind the tall counter. Perhaps it was dingier than before; and he missed the proprietor's nod of recognition, which he had subconsciously expected. After all, it had been a long time since he was last here.

Major Dougal negotiated his way through a cluster of Germans who were waiting for a table. He ducked round the counter and climbed the narrow flight of stairs to the upper room. The cracks of the linoleum were worse than they had been.

It had always puzzled him that the room upstairs was not better advertised below. It was a square and airy room with two large sash windows and a dozen tables, about half of which were occupied. A plump waitress with platinum hair and varicose veins was leaning precariously into the shaft of the dumbwaiter.

"Two tarts," she cried down to the subterranean kitchen, "and one mixed grill."

Blaines was sitting at a corner table with his back to the window. He raised a plump, pink hand like something from a butcher's slab and cut his face in two with a grin. He levered himself a few inches out of his seat and smothered Major Dougal's hand in an envelope of flesh.

"Ted, old son," he wheezed. "Have some vino."

"Hullo, Fang." The Major sat down opposite his host. There were the customary two bottles of Chianti on the table, both opened and one only half full. Blaines stuffed his cigar back in his mouth and splashed wine into their glasses.

"I'm sorry I'm late," Major Dougal said. "My train seemed to have a spot of difficulty finding Liverpool Street. How are you?"

"In the pink." Blaines leant back, causing his chair to creak ominously. He was a corpulent man with a large, turnip-shaped head and a mottled face. His hair was a mass of gray and dirty yellow curls. A cylinder of ash fell from his cigar onto his blazer. He ignored it; he was not a man who had much time for ashtrays. "You look well." He screwed up his small blue eyes. "Life among the yokels must suit you. Can't say I'd fancy it myself. But you was never what I would call a real Londoner." Colonel Blaines took a long swallow of his wine.

Major Dougal suppressed the revulsion that crept

73

through him like indigestion. He had forgotten Blaines's infallible ability to set him on edge. He cast around for a neutral topic. "Things going well at the office?"

"Things is the word," Blaines exhaled a cloud of cigar smoke. "We're so bloody mechanized these days I hardly see a human being. And when I do they call me Sir."

"I expect they still call you Fang behind your back."

Blaines stirred the phlegm in his throat with a harsh grunt. "I don't give a toss. They're all university whiz kids these days. Never heard a shot in anger. It was lucky you rang on a Monday. Lucy's day on the phones. She's the only one of our girls who's been here long enough to remember the Forester-digit routine. Christ, sometimes I feel like the last of the dinosaurs."

Major Dougal thought it was unlikely that the dragons were dying out; they were merely mutating.

Blaines hailed the passing platinum blonde. "A double mixed grill, love. What about you, Ted?"

"Steak and kidney pie, please." If the food was unchanged the pie was one of the least offensive items on the menu.

"Don't forget the ketchup, darling. And bring us another bottle."

He absentmindedly patted the broad rump of the waitress to dismiss her; she undulated appreciatively away. Blaines poured more wine into his glass and gestured with the bottle toward Major Dougal's. "Drink up. It's HM's treat today."

That sounded ominous: Fang used his expense account on other people only sparingly and for very good reason.

Their food arrived. Blaines discarded his smoldering cigar and ate with speed and concentration. Major Dougal made no attempt at conversation; dragons at feeding

74

time were not sociable animals. His own portion of pie, accompanied by classically overcooked cabbage and two curiously discolored roast potatoes, seemed minuscule beside the crowded splendors of the double mixed grill. He ate slowly—the steak demanded thorough mastication—and stared between mouthfuls at the faded color photograph of Mont-Saint-Michel behind Blaines's left shoulder; anything was better than looking at the Colonel.

Despite the difference in size between their portions, Blaines had finished before the Major had eaten a third of what was on his plate. Blaines belched and sat back. He alternately sucked his wine and picked his teeth with a broken matchstick until the vestiges of appetite deserted Major Dougal.

"Coffee," the colonel said to the waitress who was attending to the people at the next table. "And then bugger off and leave us, would you, darling."

When the coffee was on the table Blaines leant forwards. "Tell me," he said softly, "when you retired you gave me that little speech about how you wanted a permanent break. Do you still feel like that?"

Major Dougal felt himself grow tense. "As a general rule, yes. But I suppose—in the right circumstances—I might not turn down an offer of freelance work. Something small time."

"Something to supplement your pension."

In the silence that followed, Major Dougal fancied that Blaines could see past his facade—in this case the dark, well-pressed suit he had worn for Richard's funeral—to the threadbare reality beneath. It was not impossible that Fang knew all about his bungalow and his bank balance—even that the Ford Anglia had failed its MOT last month; Blaines's ability to muster background detail was one reason for his present position.

Another reason was that he had no qualms about putting whatever he amassed to effective use.

"In this case," Blaines continued, "my professional interest and your personal one may be identical. There," he added calmly, "that surprised you, didn't it?"

Major Dougal said nothing. To speak could only reveal weakness. His mind whirled like a fruit machine, trying to make the connection between a fifty-year-old murder, a World War I subaltern, Richard's suicide, and—hardest of all—what Blaines had just said.

The Colonel relit his cigar. "Corner," he mumbled. "What's your angle, Ted? I need to know."

"A friend of mine killed himself recently. He was a writer, an historian. His daughter—my goddaughter—wants to find out what was on his mind when he died. Apparently he was researching Corner for some books of his."

"Prentisse," said Blaines. "Richard and Celia. Buddy of yours right back to Normandy. Drowned himself last month. Any doubt about that?"

Major Dougal shrugged. "Odd in the sense it wasn't expected. He didn't seem the type. But then those who succeed rarely do seem the type beforehand. But Celia won't accept that it's suicide. That's why I'm here."

"I'll be frank," said Colonel Blaines, immediately arousing the Major's suspicions. "When you rang I thought, okay, I'll scratch Ted's back if he'll scratch mine. On occasion it can be useful to pull in someone off the retired list. So I sent off my skivvy to rootle around in the basement. He comes back and says the original file's been shredded and the contents transferred on to that bloody computer."

76

"A First World War file?" asked the Major incredulously. "That's not usual, is it?"

"Too right it isn't. Even the M.o.D. haven't that much time and money to waste. But it does happen sometimes. If a personal file's considered to contain material that is still sensitive, for instance. And that may not be discovered until an outside inquiry brings it to light. The theory goes that it's safer to have anything delicate tucked away in the data base rather than floating around the basement for anyone to read. Another advantage is that it's more accessible for those who are allowed to see it: if you've got something nasty in the woodshed which attracts one inquiry, others are bound to follow; you can insert those in the record as they arise without having to fiddle with bits of paper."

"Could Richard's letter have triggered the transfer?" Major Dougal pressed. "Or were there other inquiries?"

"Yes to both questions," said the Colonel, "but I don't know the chronology. That's part of the bloody problem." He lapsed into silence and broached the third bottle of Chianti

The Major protected his own glass with his hand. "The problem—?"

"The probem, old son, began to emerge when I sat in front of that horrible VDU on my desk and asked it to regurgitate what it knew about Corner. You know the routine: you tap in your name, security clearance, and password and out comes the table of contents of the file you want. Subject's name, rank, number and the vital statistics of the file—how long it is and how many appended documents there are. In Corner's case he's got twenty-seven pages and nearly as many appendices. And that is simply ridiculous for a subaltern who died in 1918. Jesus, I've got less than that. So've you, come to that."

Blaines waved a thick finger under Major Dougal's nose. "And then what happens? I ask for page one and that bastard VDU flashes up: *YOUR SECURITY CLEAR-ANCE IS INADEQUATE FOR CLASSIFIED MATE-RIAL ON THIS LEVEL.* Go straight to jail," added the Colonel with heavy sarcasm. "Do not pass Go. Do not collect two hundred pounds. Just bugger off."

"I presume the Records Division is still part of your brief," said the Major thoughtfully. "There can't be many people around with the power to override your security clearance. Could the Permanent Under-secretary?"

Blaines shook his head like a baited bull. "Larry could. But he wouldn't. Or not without buttering me up before-hand. If he queers my pitch he queers his own. You don't sneak up behind your own watchdog."

"Not usually," agreed Major Dougal. He had been too familiar with the maneuvering of Whitehall dragons to rule out the possibility entirely. "I suppose you've come up with other candidates?"

"Too many for comfort—including a good handful of semi-outsiders. Director level in Five or Six for example. Bastards, all of them." Blaines brooded for a moment over his empty wineglass. "That's the trouble with all this electronic gadgetry we got wished on us. Bloody marvel-ous what it can do. Snag is, most of us who use it don't re-alize what it *can* do. So we're at the mercy of anyone who does."

Major Dougal knew how jealously Fang guarded his territorial rights and felt a brief stab of pity for the obese Machiavelli opposite him. The unavailability of Corner's file was a worm in his apple; its contents didn't matter but their absence did. The waitress hovered and Blaines said, without looking at her, "Shag off, love," which not only achieved the desired effect but appeared to please her as well.

"Fang . . . is a response likely? Would your request for the file have been logged?"

"Shouldn't have been. I've got this little erasure button. But I wouldn't bet on it. If our bloke's got this much clout he could override that. That's one reason why I wanted to meet you here rather than the office."

"Or Saint James's Park?"

Blaines bellowed with laughter. No one talked to anyone about anything in St. James's Park if they could help it. It was an old joke—too old for Blaines to laugh at it. Major Dougal had expected it to elicit no more than a tired smile. The old man was more worried than he seemed.

The bellows subsided. Blaines wiped his mouth on the cuff of his blazer. "What puzzles me is our bloke's motive. He can't be sitting on a file that old for professional reasons. Even if there's a scandal there, who's going to care? It's got cobwebs on it. So more likely it's personal, which makes it a lot more dodgy."

"Because less predictable."

"Spot on. By the way, at least you're not involved. I had a word with Lucy on the way out: there's no record of your call this morning. Thank God she's not a machine."

Major Dougal felt relieved—the possibility had occurred to him. Relief made him generous, and he outlined what he knew about Corner—the encyclopedia, the possible link with an old murder case and Prentisse's unsubstantiated suspicion that the subaltern's commitment to socialism was greater than his loyalty to the army.

"That's all we need," said Blaines. "A bloody political

79

angle." He busied himself with another cigar. "The way I see it," he said between puffs of his cigar, "we've got two lines of approach. I can sniff around the department and try to find the source of that security override. I've got my tame technicians too. You can do the legwork on the outside. Try and find someone who remembers Corner. It's just possible, man."

"I could contact the regimental history association," suggested Major Dougal. "It might help if you could arrange for me to have some sort of accreditation. I'd prefer it under another name, naturally."

"So would I." The Colonel's chuckle was uncomfortably like a snarl. "I'll get something in the post this afternoon." Blaines pulled out his wallet and extracted ten twenty-pound notes. "Expenses. I'll see you get the usual freelance rate. Thank God for petty cash."

Major Dougal reluctantly scooped up the notes. The action marked the point of no return, as Blaines would be perfectly aware. "What's the contacting procedure? Will you ring me?"

Blaines nodded.

"Then perhaps I should mention that my son is at home. It's possible he might answer."

"I remember—Willam." Blaines's porcine eyes squinted through the smoke. He said nothing more for a moment, leaving the Major to wonder exactly what he did remember.

"One more thing, Ted. Did Corner leave any dependents?"

"A wife and a son who was born posthumously. She died in 1919."

Once again, Fang's face split into that terrible grin. "Then here's a little item you may find useful. The table of contents of a file usually includes an indication of pension status. Whether there was one. Corner's didn't. What does that suggest to you?"

There could be several explanations," said the Major slowly. "The most likely one is that he was court-martialed."

9

THE DOOR BURST open with such force that it bounced against the side table by the doorway. The table and telephone upon it keeled over.

William was on his feet before the telephone hit the floor. Celia wondered how his reflexes came to be so sharp.

"Sorry," said the vicar. The metal tray swayed dangerously in his hands. "The door used to stick, you see, so I got into the habit of using my shoulder on it. Oh *blast.*"

He set down the tray on the hearth rug. The three mugs were cylindrical islands in a gray, circular sea. Celia passed him a wad of paper handkerchiefs. If this went on, she would need to buy another box before the day was out. He mopped up the coffee, tossing the soggy tissues one by one into the empty grate. Meanwhile William restored the table and the telephone to their original positions.

"Thank you," said the vicar. He was in his early thirties, Celia guessed, but doomed to remain perpetually adolescent as far as his muscular coordination was concerned. He was small and skinny, with a large forehead and a receding hairline. He looked like an intelligent horse.

"Do you need another tissue?" she asked.

82

The vicar wiped his fingers on his faded corduroy trousers. "Not at present, thanks. I expect I shall. Inanimate objects never behave themselves with me. Do either of you have sugar? I forgot to bring it."

Celia shook her head. Neither of them had milk either, but it was too late to do anything about that.

He handed the mugs to his guests and sat down in the armchair facing Celia's across the fireplace. William was on the sofa between them.

"You're lucky to catch me in," the vicar said. "I should have been at the Women's Institute this afternoon, but they had to postpone the meeting. What can I do for you?"

William took one sip of his coffee and hurriedly put it down on the side table. "Mr. Davis," he said bravely, "I'm afraid we're here under false pretenses. We're not connected with Meals on Wheels."

Mr. Davis scratched his furrowed forehead. "Silly of me. The Council said they were sending someone around today and I assumed, because I didn't recognize you . . . It's so easy to jump to conclusions."

"It doesn't matter," said Celia gently. She had a sudden and wholly maternal desire to stroke the vicar's forehead in an attempt to smooth away those creases. "We're trying to trace one of your parishioners—an old lady who used to live at Boreham Hall. When we went up there we found the house was empty, so we thought we'd try the vicarage."

"It's a depressing house, isn't it?" said Mr. Davis. "Gives me the willies. Red brick and rhododendron, and it always seems to be raining there. Silly name, too—it's just a suburban villa transplanted into the depths of Suffolk. Are you relatives?"

"Not exactly." Celia was conscious of William's warning glance but decided to ignore it. Why should he call all the shots? "We bought a secondhand encyclopedia, which happened to have some old letters in one of the volumes. Rather personal stuff. We hoped we could return them. The bookseller told us he'd got them at an auction at Boreham Hall."

"Oh dear. It looks as if you may have had a wasted journey. There were two old ladies living in the house; one of them died and the other sold up and went to live with her niece in South Africa. I've got her address, if that's any use. I suppose it rather depends which one of the letters belonged to."

"What were their names?" Celia asked. "The letters don't make it clear."

"The one in South Africa is Maud Bench. She was a sort of nurse-companion to the one who died, Mrs. Hinton. It was quite a tragedy, the way she died."

"Hinton?" William interrupted. "Do you know her first name?"

"Beatrice Mary," said Mr. Davis promptly. "I only found out because of the gravestone. She'd been in the village for donkey's years—she arrived just after the war, I think. But Maud came to live with her quite recently. It was just before I came to the parish. Six or seven years ago."

"It's an old encyclopedia," said Celia thoughtfully. "I suppose it's more likely that the letters belonged to Mrs. Hinton. Did you know her well?"

"Not really. Neither of them was a regular churchgoer. I saw more of Miss Bench—Mrs. Hinton was practically housebound for the last eighteen months of her life. She had a reputation for being something of a recluse. Which made that business about the television program seem rather strange."

Celia wondered if she had misheard. "I don't quite—"

"You wouldn't know," said Mr. Davis with a touch of smugness. "Of course not. I didn't, until after Mrs. Hinton was dead. Miss Bench told me that she had been approached by one of the independent television companies. They were planning a series on old murder trials. It seems that Mrs. Hinton was involved in one in the thirties. I imagine she was a witness of some sort. It's strange, you can live with these people for years and never really know what makes them tick. Miss Bench hadn't heard about it before. I gather Mrs. Hinton had agreed to be interviewed. But then it was too late."

"How did she die?" asked William.

"Smoking," said the vicar sternly. "Smoking in bed. It's such a wantonly suicidal habit. Mrs. Hinton must have been in her eighties. She had a weak heart and bronchial trouble; and she still smoked thirty untipped cigarettes a day. One night she fell asleep with a lighted cigarette in her hand. It fell on the eiderdown, which was made of some synthetic material so it went up like a torch. She was well on the way to being suffocated when her heart gave out on her. Luckily Miss Bench smelt the smoke and was able to put the fire out before it spread. But it was too late for poor Mrs. Hinton."

"It's a lesson to us all." William's tone was grave. Celia glanced swiftly at him in disapproval.

"Life," said the vicar with a professional glint in his eyes, "sometimes reminds me of a rabbit warren. Every now and then death introduces a few stoats. It seems frighteningly random, doesn't it?"

"Oh, I don't know." William pulled out his cigarettes. "I'd say that death often seems frighteningly well organized. That's the trouble."

10

CELIA KNEW IT meant trouble when she heard Margaret's laugh. She had come straight back after dropping William at the bungalow. Major Dougal wasn't there, though he had left a note to say he had to pop up to London and wasn't sure when he would be back. Celia had decided to go back home—she had to get down to clearing her father's study sooner or later. She had arranged to ring William after dinner.

She heard Margaret's laugh just as she was about to insert her key in the front door. It had that girlish trill that her stepmother usually adopted with men of whom she approved. Celia stiffened. She glanced back at the Deux Chevaux, which she had left parked on the road, since she was planning to go out later in the evening. She was sorely tempted to leap into it and drive as far as possible from Plumford.

The garage and an area of hard standing lay at the side of the house. Celia, having resisted the temptation to flee, walked with self-conscious stealth toward it to verify a suspicion that had sprung up in her mind.

She was right: in front of the garage door was parked a bright green Volkswagen. Anger jolted through her like an electrical charge. She squared her shoulders and went into the house by the back entrance, slamming the door behind her in memory of all the times that Margaret had asked her to close doors quietly. Before she reached the sitting room she knew she had been heard—the conversation had stopped.

As she entered the room, Jim stood up. He and Margaret had been comfortably ensconced in the armchairs by the fireplace, a tea tray positioned between them.

"Celia . . ." His voice died away. He took a step toward her and stopped. "How are you?"

"Fine, thank you," she said tartly. She resented the implication that there might be anything wrong with her in the first place. "Is there any tea in the pot? Shall I get another cup?"

"No need, dear. I brought one for you." Margaret bent forward, put her hand on the teapot but made no move to pour. Celia realized she was waiting to see how Jim would greet her.

Celia preemptively sat down. Jim remained standing, swaying uncertainly. She felt a sudden, physical revulsion at the sight of him—in particular, at the fold of flesh that was beginning to bulge above the waistline of his gray flannel trousers and the blunt nose with the hair-fringed chasms of its nostrils.

Margaret poured the tea and handed it to Jim to pass to Celia. "It's nice of Jim to call in," she remarked reprovingly, without looking at her stepdaughter. "Not easy for a teacher to get away during the week in termtime."

"That's all too true, I'm afraid." Jim carefully avoided touching Celia's hand during the transfer of the cup and saucer. "I did have the Computer Club after school, but Mick said he'd look after them. He sends his love, by the way. So does Janice."

"That's nice," said Celia. Jim had chosen to relay the

87

good wishes of the two colleagues she liked least: Mick was a young toady who had firmly hitched himself to what he considered to be Jim's rising star; Janice was in the PE department and Celia had every sympathy with the kids who called her the Physical Jerk.

Jim sat down heavily in his chair and rummaged in the inside pocket of his tweed jacket. "I did have a list . . ." Of course he did, thought Celia: he had one for every occasion. ". . . Ah, here we are. I wanted to ask about the dry-cleaning ticket for my interview suit; I can't find it. And Maggie wanted to know if you still thought *Othello* was a good choice for Five C. She wondered if the stereotypes of violence might be a little too heavy for them. And the headmistress had a chat with me this morning. She said—no, hinted—that your absence was rather inconvenient . . . Don't get we wrong, but I think we have to think of the long term. She could be important where references are concerned."

Celia finished her tea before answering. "To answer your questions in order. You put the dry-cleaning ticket in the jug on the end of the dining-room mantelpiece. Five C contain the Jones brothers and the Wilson gang, so they probably know more about violence than Shakespeare ever did. And, last but not least, I don't give a damn what the headmistress thinks."

It was Margaret who finally broke the awkward silence. "Celia," she cooed, "we are all quite naturally upset at present. We must make allowances. But Jim *is* right. You have to think ahead. You have the rest of your life to lead. And what you do inevitably affects Jim. We mustn't be selfish, must we?"

"I know Richard's death was a great tragedy," Jim said in the solemn tone he used for morning assembly. "But we mustn't lose our sense of proportion."

As he leaned forward, smiling sympathetically, Celia wondered how she had ever managed to go to bed with this earnest stranger in front of her. It was suddenly a question of aesthetics, purged of emotion and devoid of any solution.

"There's no 'we' about it," she said. "In fact I think I've just got my sense of proportion back."

"Has William Dougal got anything to do with this?" asked Margaret sharply. "I knew it was unwise for you to see so much of him again." Her mouth clamped tight and she glanced toward Jim. Celia saw complicity, or at least lack of surprise, on Jim's face, and realized that the subject of William Dougal had been well ventilated before she arrived.

Jim cleared his throat uneasily. "The point is, love, we've made a big investment in the future. *Our* future. Not just teaching, but in the house."

"I know." Celia avoided his eyes. She had known that meeting Jim again wouldn't be easy and having Margaret as a witness to what she wanted to say made it twice as difficult.

"I'm sure we can talk this through, if we give it a chance," Jim said. "Maybe I've been too involved in school. I've not been supportive enough."

For an instant Celia wavered. She saw a vision of blameless domesticity stretching far into the future: her job gave way to children of her own and, once they were old enough, to suitable voluntary activities. It was a secure and protected prospect: and it was expected of her.

Then Margaret made her presence felt: "You must be sensible, dear—"

"Sensible?" Celia's echo was considerably louder than the original. "I don't want to be sensible. I've been sensible all my life." She stood up, rummaging through her bag for the car keys. She was conscious of two things: that she was acting like a self-dramatizing adolescent and that she was thoroughly enjoying the experience.

"What are you doing?" asked Margaret.

"I'm going out. I don't know when I'll be back." She turned toward Jim. "This evening I'm going to write a letter of resignation. Don't worry, I'll work out my notice. Also, I want my share of the house. I don't mind whether you buy me out or we put it on the market. I think I'll put that in writing too. It should be in the post tomorrow."

Celia walked briskly out of the house before the others could say anything. She felt like a cured cripple who had donated her crutches to more deserving people.

As the car's engine fired, she hoped the cure wouldn't turn out to be a temporary phenomenon, like so much faith-healing.

The trouble with freedom, Celia thought a little later, was that it was much easier to strive for it than to know what to do with it when you had it. In the end she stopped at a telephone box and rang an old schoolfriend who now ran one of Plumford's five flourishing antique shops. The friend asked her to dinner, which in the event proved to consist of several very large gin and tonics and a bottle of Beaujolais, accompanied by unattractive paté and some stale French bread.

Those few hours were an oasis. It was a relief to obliterate, if only temporarily, the last few days under modified memories of the Lower Sixth and scandalous biographies of the subsequent careers of their classmates. The friend made an immense effort and managed to avoid the subject of William.

Celia left a little after nine, impelled by a hazy conviction that she should be doing something. The stairs down from the friend's flat made her giggle: they rippled beneath her feet like a maverick escalator. The fresh air hit her like a whip. She swayed against the doorpost and realized that it might be wiser to leave the car and walk.

But in which direction should she walk? She made herself more comfortable against the doorpost and considered the options. Sometime she would have to go home—if any house that Margaret owned could be called that. But not now: she needed to be able to think straight if she was going to face her stepmother. At least Jim must have gone back by now; the evening's marking would always take precedence over his personal problems—and, for that matter, hers as well. She had, of course, promised to ring the Dougals. She decided instead to call on them. The walk would sober her up, and she would perhaps be able to pick up the car on the way back.

The walk had the desired effect, though it took much longer than she would have believed possible. A drunken farmer propositioned her outside the Angel; the experience was distasteful enough to shake some of the alcoholic torpor from her muscles. The hill up to the bungalow had become forbiddingly steep, but she got round this by pretending she was a sailing dinghy tacking against the wind.

She paused at Major Dougal's front gate, made wary by the sense that something was different. It took her a moment to work out what it was: the Ford Anglia was no longer parked in the drive.

William opened the door, his face brightening as he saw her.

Celia forgot her carefully rehearsed explanation for her presence. "I think I need some coffee."

"By the smell of you," said William as he took her coat, "you need quite a lot of it."

They went into the kitchen. Celia sat at the table while William made the coffee. The silence between them was so comfortable that she felt her eyelids drooping. She jerked herself back to the present when William set the jug on the table.

"My father's not back yet, but he shouldn't be long. He rang just after you left this afternoon. Said he hoped to catch the eight o'clock train."

"What's he doing up there?"

"Your guess is as good as mine. He just said someone called Frederick Forester might ring, and if so I was to tell him which train my father would be on."

William lit a cigarette and the silence returned for a few minutes. As Celia pulled the coffee jug toward her for a refill, she said:

"Jim was waiting for me when I got back. He and Margaret had their heads together. I told him I was handing in my notice at school, and that I was leaving him."

"And are you?" William's face was expressionless.

Celia ignored the question. "And then I went and got drunk with Meg. Do you remember Meg? Dark hair and giggles."

"The one like a Pre-Raphaelite with a brace on her teeth?"

"That's it. Except she hasn't got a brace any more, and I don't think Pre-Raphaelite women went in for dreadlocks."

William exhaled a long lungful of smoke. "You really are leaving him and the school?"

92

"Yes," Celia yawned. "Probably. I'll think about it to-morrow. What do you think?"

"That's neither here nor there." William smiled. "But—"

The sound of a key in the lock of the front door cut off his words. Major Dougal appeared in the kitchen door-way. He nodded to Celia, acknowledging her presence as economically as possible.

"William," he said with a frown. "Where the devil's the car gone?"

"It's at the garage." William stubbed out his cigarette and reached for a third mug. "I asked them to collect it this afternoon. Coffee?"

The Major took the mug automatically. "But I told you, I've already had an estimate from them. I haven't the money to get it through its MOT test."

"Yes, but I have. It's a sort of contribution to the house-keeping. Sugar?"

Celia was aware that more than the sugar was passed. The subject was shelved, at least until Celia was out of the room. Major Dougal blew his nose loudly.

The conversation turned to a neutral topic—the day's activities. Celia quickly outlined what they had discovered. "It's a dead end, really," she concluded. "Mrs. Hinton was almost certainly Mrs. Landis, the wife of the murderer, though we've no absolute proof. Her death came just at the moment she was planning to talk about the case, after fifty years of silence. Like Daddy's suicide, her accident could have been murder."

"There's no evidence," said William. "Except that if the deaths were unrelated, they add up to a hell of a coincidence."

"What about this Bench woman?" asked the Major.

"We can write to her," Celia said. "The vicar gave us

93

her address in Durban. But I doubt if she'll be able to help—I got the impression that she would have told the vicar if she'd known anything. She seemed to be the chatty type. Did you have any luck?"

The Major cleared his throat. Celia looked curiously at him: he seemed different—less tired, less old, and perhaps less frank. "My day wasn't particularly fruitful," he said. "I saw a few old friends. Two points emerged: Corner may have been court-martialed; and it's just possible that his career may be covered by the Official Secrets Act. I don't know why, but it can hardly matter—his life or death can have no connection with the murder."

This, thought Celia, was the man who yesterday lunchtime was proclaiming that Corner was the key, with the fervor of an Old Testament prophet. She glanced at William and saw his eyes flicker in response. That uncomfortable telepathy was in operation again: *Something strange here,* their eyes agreed, *but let it ride for the moment.*

The Major shifted uncomfortably in his seat and became absorbed in squeezing more coffee from the pot.

"So that's as far as you can go?" inquired William.

"Probably," agreed Major Dougal. "You see the records for executed soldiers come under the Judge Advocate General's department; at present there is a seventy-five-year ban on publication. I believe they are thinking of relaxing it to thirty years, but the new rule will take time to come into effect. And even so there may be some exceptions."

"Why?" asked Celia suspiciously.

"Well, I suppose in more recent cases court-martial transcripts might contain intelligence material. Or some might be kept out of circulation for humanitarian reasons."

94

"To prevent relatives from being upset?" Celia smiled sweetly at her godfather. "Like hearing about the unmentionable things that grandpa did with the regimental poodle?"

"Perhaps." Major Dougal looked unhappy.

"One thing's for sure," William said. "No one outside the department will know the criteria for maintaining an embargo."

The Major nodded. "By the way," he remarked offhandedly, "I have to go up to town again tomorrow. That's the trouble with asking favors—the recipient has to scratch a back or two in return."

On Tuesday morning Celia awoke with a thick head. The ringing of the telephone was cutting into it like a slicer through cheese. She looked at her watch and saw it was already 9.45. Margaret must be out, which was just as well after the row they had had before going to bed.

Last night presented itself to her in a flash, like a full-length documentary compressed to a single frame. She swung her legs from under the duvet and padded barefooted down to the kitchen. One hand fumbled with the telephone while the other tried to rub the bleariness from her eyes.

"Celia?" It was William's voice on the other end of the line.

"Uh. Hullo. You got me out of bed." She felt aggrieved: one of the advantages of freedom was surely being able to choose when you got up; and William had ruined the enjoyment of her first morning. It wasn't as if they had arranged to do anything today.

"Listen. My father had gone out by the time I got up. Presumably to London. But there was a phone call for him a few minutes ago. It was a woman with one of those gymkhana voices. She asked for him by name. I said he was out for the day and could I take a message? She asked who I was—and it was then I realized she was crying. Then she said: *Tell your father Frederick Forester has gone west on the District Line.*"

"Forester?" Celia felt the palm of her hand grow sweaty against the plastic of the telephone receiver. "That was the bloke your father said might ring yesterday."

"Right. I asked who to say had called, and she said: *Tell him it was Lucy but he mustn't try and contact me.* Then she gave a sort of wail and put the phone down."

"Oh God. *Gone west*—is that another one of the vicar's stoats, d'you think? What the hell's Uncle Ted got himself into?"

"I don't know. The way the woman was crying . . . Oh *God.*" William sounded desperately worried; Celia's memory stirred abruptly, reminding her of the evening ten years before when she had told William she was pregnant. "The thing is," he continued, "does he know what's going on? And is this why he was being so bloody mysterious last night? Maybe he expected something like this to happen, and was trying to keep us out of it."

Celia responded to William's tone rather than his words. "I'll be over as soon as I can. Say fifteen minutes, okay, love?"

As she put the phone down she found William's panic was beginning to infect her as well. She had taken it for granted all her life that Uncle Ted was entirely what he seemed: a modest, upright old soldier, as reliable as Eddystone Lighthouse.

11

THE DRIVE FROM Manchester Picadilly to the nursing home near Altrincham took nearly an hour. The journey would have been shorter if Major Dougal had been less confident of his knowledge of Manchester's one-way system. It would have been shorter still if he had taken a taxi; but that, he judged, would have introduced an unnecessary witness to his movements.

Moreover, the hiring of a car was financially painless. Two credit cards had been included in the kit that had arrived from Blaines in that morning's post, along with a driving license and no less than three identity cards. The latter were designed to cover most eventualities. The rather grand one, with a Technicolor representation of the royal arms and phraseology reminiscent of a passport's, was meant for more impressionable members of the public. The white one was smaller and more restrained; it accredited the bearer to the Ministry of Defense and included a ten-year-old photograph of Major Dougal; this was for official and military consumption. The third—a green rectangle of laminated plastic—was the least obtrusive of all; some of its details could only be revealed under ultraviolet light; this card was only to be used as a last resort if he fell foul of the security services.

All the documents referred to him as Major Charles A. Harrell. He could dimly remember Harrell—a thin man with half-moon glasses who had pseudonymously blown himself up while assisting a former colonial regime that officially did not exist. If Blaines had had more time to provide it, the cover would have been better. But in the circumstances Harrell should do very nicely.

Old habits had swiftly reasserted themselves. Major Dougal found he was driving as fast as possible within the speed limits. He kept a constant check on his rear mirror. It was unlikely that Corner's mysterious protector had rumbled Blaines; and even more unlikely that Blaines's meeting with himself had been noted; but caution cost nothing.

In Altrincham he was forced to ask a policeman for directions to the road he wanted. It was a broad, tree-lined avenue with wide pavements bordered by high brick walls, behind which could be glimpsed more trees and large, well-spaced houses. They looked as if they had been built for Victorian magnates, with gardens to match their owners' territorial ambitions. Since then the neighborhood had changed in character—the Major had driven past at least two private schools and one misleadingly named country club—but it had not moved down-market.

The wrought-iron gates of the Bognor Grange Retirement Home were open. Major Dougal went up the graveled drive, which twisted around two shrubberies and a rockery to create an illusion of length, and parked by the front porch. He turned off the engine and spent a minute looking around him.

The overall impression was one of wealth—of solid, unostentatious comfort, which made no concession to considerations of cost and taste. The trim lawns were dotted with carefully manicured flower beds. Even the trees looked tidy and upright, as if on their best behavior. Major Dougal's hire car was dwarfed by the other occupants of the drive—a Bentley, a BMW, and a Mercedes whose polished paintwork gleamed in the midday sunlight. The house itself—a fussy Victorian pastiche of architectural styles to which a modern wing had been added—was equally well maintained. The porch—a two-storied erection with richly ornamented tiles and enough stained glass for a small parish church—probably featured an oubliette for any tradesman who didn't know his place.

Major Dougal left the haven of his car, mounted the steps and rang the bell. The door was opened by a pretty young blonde with a well-scrubbed face and a uniform that simultaneously suggested the nurse and the parlor maid. The Major removed his hat.

"Good morning. My name is Harrell. I believe that Mr. Walker is expecting me."

The blonde ushered him into a large, well-carpeted hall. "You have an appointment, sir? It is nearly lunchtime."

"Yes," said Major Dougal firmly. "I rang Miss Garner-Brown earlier today."

The prim set of the girl's mouth relaxed. "Oh, if Matron knows . . . One moment, sir, I'll go and fetch her. Do take a seat."

Miss Garner-Brown was a large, capable-looking woman with carefully coifed iron gray hair, a twin-set, and an enormous pair of glasses of baroque design. She advanced toward him with her hand outstretched.

"Major Harrell," she purred—her voice was unexpectedly soft but by no means gentle, "how do you do. We couldn't persuade you to defer your visit until after lunch, I suppose? Our residents are so attached to their little routines."

Major Dougal swiftly sized her up: an autocrat whose power in her own domain it would be wise to respect, but not a person without vanities. The glasses were a give-away.

"Miss Garner-Brown, I do appreciate your concern, but the matter could be urgent." He was damned if he was going to hang about to suit the old bag's conven-ience. "I mentioned on the phone that my business with Mr. Walker was official. In fact—and this is strictly in confidence—it relates to the defense of the realm." He pitched his voice so low that she had to bend toward him. As he finished speaking he handed her his most ornate identity card.

Her eyes widened as she examined it, and a faint flush crept into her cheeks. The Major held out his hand for it before she had finished, as if the document was too pre-cious to be let out of his possession for a moment.

"Of course, Major Harrell." Miss Garner-Brown glanced conspiratorially around the wide, empty expanse of the hall to check they were alone. "I had no *idea* that Mr. Walker—"

"I must stress that the nature of my visit must be kept between ourselves. It's a standard precaution, you under-stand."

"But of course, Major." Miss Garner-Brown's expres-sion conveyed that she was no stranger to the rituals and romance of cloak-and-dagger work. "I'll take you to Mr. Walker. He's in the conservatory. I'll see that you're not disturbed."

100

"That would be most kind." Major Dougal followed the matron's tall, upright figure through a large sitting room, where half a dozen elderly people forsook their crosswords and preprandial sherries to examine him, and ushered him into the sun-filled conservatory beyond. The room was empty except for a figure in a wheelchair facing away from them.

"Mr. Walker," cooed Miss Garner-Brown, "we have a visitor." She added in a lower voice to the Major: "I did mention your phone call to him after breakfast, but I'm afraid his memory isn't what it was."

"Either *you* have a visitor," said Mr. Walker, without turning his sparsely covered head, "or *I* have a visitor. One or t'other." His paper-thin voice had a Mancunian accent; it reminded Major Dougal of the rustle of dead leaves.

Miss Garner-Brown bent over Mr. Walker and ruthlessly hoisted up a pillow. "He's come all the way from London," she said brightly. "His name is Major Harrell." She straightened the collar of Mr. Walker's dressing gown and smoothed the rug over his knees. "It's very important, so mind you be a good boy and answer his questions."

She gave Mr. Walker one last pat. "I'll be in the sitting room if you want me," she whispered loudly to Major Dougal.

The Major opened the door for her and made sure it was properly closed behind her. He returned to the wheelchair and got his first good look at its occupant. Mr. Walker had once been a big man, but age had shrunk him. Deep wrinkles fissured his pallid skin. His blue eyes were faded and watery. One of his thin, almost translucent hands picked at the rug on his lap.

101

"It's very good of you to see me, sir, especially at such short notice." Major Dougal pulled over a chair and sat down. "As you know, my name's Harrell and—"

"It's a conspiracy," Mr. Walker interrupted. "They're all in it. My daughter put me in here and they treat me like a child. Think I'm senile. That's not very clever, is it? I feel just the same as I always did. It's just my health isn't so good these days. It's crazy: I have to pay good money to be treated like a baby. Everyone wants money. Doctors are worse than most. Your lot want a week's wages for spending ten minutes with me. Should've stuck with the National Health."

Major Dougal seized his opportunity. "Mr. Walker, I'm not a doctor; I'm from the Ministry of Defense. I would just like to ask you a few questions."

"I thought she said you were a doctor . . . " Mr. Walker sucked in his cheeks over his toothless gums. Major Dougal waited patiently for him to assimilate the idea. "War Office, eh?" The eyes were suddenly alert with suspicion. "You trying to make a monkey out of me?"

"No, sir." The Major produced his passport to other people's fantasies. "Here's my identity card."

Mr. Walker turned it over in his hands. His fingertips slowly stroked both sides. His face remained expressionless. The card slipped out of his hands, slid down the rug and fell to the floor. "What does it matter?" he said helplessly as the Major retrieved it. "My eyes aren't good enough for reading now."

"I'm sorry." Major Dougal meant it. "Believe me, I am."

"Don't ever let them put you in a Home, young man," Mr. Walker hissed with surprising vigor. "When the time comes, you take my tip: get a bottle of Scotch and a few dozen sleeping pills. Best way out for everyone."

No one had called Major Dougal "young man" for at least twenty years; he was flattered. He also thought Mr. Walker's advice might prove sound. Mixed with this was a growing sense of desperation: was Walker too far gone to be of any use to him?

"We're working on a historical project, Mr. Walker. Your reminiscences might be of great value to us. Your old regiment gave us your name and address."

"My old regiment don't exist," Walker said sharply. "When I came out in 'forty-six it were called—"

"I know. Military reorganization is always a mixed blessing," interrupted Major Dougal. He had to channel this conversation: otherwise it could flood out into a great, uncharted sea of memory. " 'Forty-six was the end of your second spell in the army. I'm interested in the first."

A grin spread across Walker's face. "I were underage," he cackled. "I fooled 'em proper. You want to know how I did it?"

"In May 1918," continued the Major remorselessly, "you and your battalion were resting. Then came the German offensive against the French Sixth Army, which was supported by four British divisions. Your battalion was unexpectedly warned for duty on the line. You were a corporal. In the same company—"

"Oh bloody hell. The noise. Those bombardments were like devils dancing in your brain."

"—In the same company was a subaltern called Corner. Remember him?"

" 'Course I remember. When you get old there's nowt else to do. The funny thing is, it gets easier the further back you go. Damned if I can recall what I had for breakfast today or the details of when I sold the construction business four years ago. But that bloody war's as

103

clear as if it were yesterday. Or as clear as yesterday used to be, if you follow me. Lord, I could tell you how to dismantle a Lewis, step by step, if I wanted to."

"Can you tell me about Corner?"

"The pinko? HP we used to call him, after Hyde Park. Too matey by half." Walker chuckled. "He got what was coming to him, at any rate. At that stage of the war they were really scraping the barrel for officers. Poor old HP didn't have what it took: he knew it and so did we. You could tell the other officers didn't like him. Neither fish nor flesh nor good red herring, that were the trouble."

"He was generally disliked?" prompted Major Dougal.

The thin shoulders shrugged, almost imperceptibly beneath the heavy dressing gown. "*We* didn't dislike him. He was a soft touch. Agree to anything, he would, if you let him give you one of his pamphlets. Couldn't give an order to save his life. It was always, 'Please, Corporal, would you mind . . . ' Poor sod. He were one of those nervy blokes. We knew he wouldn't last long in France. That sort never did."

"What happened to him?"

But Walker was not to be hurried. An audience that actually listened to him was a rarity to be savored. Major Dougal heard a great deal about conditions in the trenches, the Chemin des Dames, and the biographies of what seemed to be everyone in Walker's company, with the solitary exception of Corner.

Finally Walker returned to May 1918 and the sudden order to the front. ". . . We entrained around midnight. The battalion had been hanging around the station for at least an hour. And Corner weren't there. Then just at the last moment he turns up between a couple of MPs, looking very sorry for himself. They took him along to the col-

104

onel. Now I had a mate who were an orderly with battalion HQ, and he were near enough to overhear what happened when they met. MP sergeant says they found him sulking in a room above an *estaminet* with a suitcase full of civvies. Corner says no he weren't; he'd been locked in the room and he didn't know how the suitcase got there. And the colonel sort of looks down his nose and has him placed under arrest. We never saw him again."

Major Dougal let out his breath. So Blaines had been right. Desertion was a common enough offense, especially in that theatre of war. Nearly 350 men had been executed after courts-martial during World War I, and most of them for the military crime of desertion.

". . . We heard a few weeks later he'd been shot. Surprised us—they shot a lot of people but usually not officers. Maybe the brass thought knocking off a subaltern would show how fair-minded they were, shooting one of their own. Except Corner weren't one of their own and that's probably why they chose him to make an example of. They'd've done better to send the yellow ones home. I remember a mick we had who tried to desert once . . . "

It might so easily have been a put-up job. Very few people need have been involved. Medical boards were used as rubber stamps. A capital sentence would go all the way up to the Commander-in-Chief for confirmation, but no one would consider mercy if the batallion commander's report was sufficiently damning. Certainly Haig wouldn't. Courts-martial, even in the later stage of the war, were scarcely models of legal justice. If Corner was not only an unsatisfactory soldier but a Socialist who was believed to be actively damaging the war effort, a fixed court-martial might have seemed the ideal solution. Leaks to Snowden and the press would be blocked; the

105

troops' morale would be raised by the knowledge that an officer was subject to the same discipline as themselves; and Corner would be permanently discredited.

It was merely supposition, Major Dougal conceded to himself, based on an interpretation of hearsay recollected from the other end of a lifetime. But it did hang together. If Corner's file contained even a hint that his death had been due to conspiracy, it explained why someone was anxious to keep it under wraps, even after all these years.

But surely not anxious enough to kill? How could Richard Prentisse and Mrs. Hinton have needed to die?

"Hey!" Walker was glaring at him. "You're not listening. You're like everyone else. Don't forget, young man, I'm paying your bills. I want some medical attention or you won't get a penny out of me."

Major Dougal soothed the old man and reorientated him. He stayed for another ten minutes, methodically checking that Walker had no further information that might be useful. He succeeded in extracting the names of both the company commander and the battalion commander; both men must have been privy to any conspiracy—and both men had been killed before the Armistice.

It was hardly surprising, Major Dougal reflected as he gave a farewell shake to the leather-wrapped bundle of bones on the end of the old man's right arm. After so much time, what could Blaines expect but a series of dead ends?

Miss Garner-Brown herself showed Major Dougal to the front door.

"Well," she said archly, "you must come again. You've given Mr. Walker quite an appetite for lunch. He's got a bit of color in his cheeks too."

The Major held out his hand and made a wordless sound, which, he hoped, expressed pleasure at Mr. Walker's improved health, gratitude for Miss Garner-Brown's cooperation, and a deeply regretted but urgent need to be elsewhere.

Nevertheless, he lingered in the porch after the door closed behind him, staring at the gleaming row of cars. Part of his mind was doing its job: assessing the likelihood that Miss Garner-Brown would pry the purpose of his visit from Mr. Walker, and deciding that it wasn't worth worrying about. The rest of him could not help thinking of whiskey and a bottle of sleeping pills. Walker was right. He and most of those pampered hulks were living in a half-world. They lingered in the anteroom of death, incapable of retreat and afraid of advancing. Better a dead end than a dying end.

Major Dougal unlocked his car and slid gingerly onto the hot plastic of the driver's seat. As he fumbled with the ignition, he realized that only two leads remained to be investigated. Then Blaines would be off his back.

That of course was his most important goal. He knew from experience that unwarranted interference with an M.o.D. file was just the sort of incident to trigger a civil war among the dragons. He was less worried for himself than for William and Celia. Those young innocents had no idea of what could happen when dragons were brawling. No one was allowed to be an innocent bystander when national security could be said to be at stake.

12

CELIA SAT AT the Dougals' kitchen table and wrote two
letters, one to her headmistress and the other to Jim. She
wasn't sure why she had stayed—there was nothing she
could do to help William. While she wrote he wandered
through the bungalow, picking up and discarding activities. He reminded her of the woman who has everything,
looking for something else in a clothes shop.

He made a pot of tea but forgot to pour it. He glanced
at yesterday's crossword, did three clues with indecent
speed and threw the newspaper in the wastepaper basket. He read a few pages of a crime novel. At last, and to
Celia's great relief, he came through to the kitchen and
perched on the edge of the table.

Celia welcomed the excuse to stop writing. "I've done
the first one," she said. "The second one's harder."

"How far have you got?"

"Dear Jim, I really think it's better . . . "

William grinned. "It's a start. Just give it to him
straight and don't beat around the bush . . . you're not
having second thoughts?"

Celia shook her head and tried to gauge William's reaction by his expression. Pleasure? Relief? Disappoint-

ment? It was as hard to guess his feelings as it was to know what she wanted them to be. He began to kick one of the table legs.

"Stop it. You're acting like the parent of a teenager who's stayed out after midnight for the first time."

"I know it's stupid," William retorted. He slipped off the table with a jerk and lit a cigarette. His mouth twisted. "You could call it filial piety. I'm making up for lost time."

"He'll be all right." Celia changed subjects; if it had been gears there would have been a grating noise. "Is there anything more we can do, beside write to that Bench woman?"

William took a minute to answer. "I can only think of two things. We could try to trace the kids—the nephew who was Corner's son and the Landis boy."

"The nephew must have been about twelve in 1931, but the son was just a baby. If he was alive you'd think he'd turn up for his mother's funeral. I'm sure the vicar would have mentioned it if he had."

"If they are alive they could well be living under different names."

Celia fiddled with her biro. Her father was dead: the memory of that unassailable fact returned again and kicked her in the stomach. What was the point of trying to find out why? If there was a why. Delving into the past seemed about as productive as trying to excavate a quicksand. All you could do with a shovelful of oblivion was return it whence it came and hope you didn't get sucked down in the process.

"Where would we start?" she asked. "Find their birth certificates?"

"I'm not sure we're the best people to look." William

109

ground out his cigarette. "I think we should subcontract it. It's a job for an expert."

"A private detective? I couldn't afford one."

"Not a private detective. And there's no need to worry about money."

Celia felt herself flushing. "I'm not taking any more money from you."

"I'm not giving it to you." William glanced down at her and said in a gentler voice: "I've got a stake in finding out what happened to Uncle Richard. It's for me as much as you."

Celia also heard what he didn't say: *There's no way you can stop me.* Where did all this money come from? Once more she was aware of that huge unknown hinterland of William's life.

"I know just the person," he went on as if the matter was settled. "An old friend who's a freelance journalist. He's a very efficient ferret and more or less trustworthy. And I happen to know he's between jobs at present. What do you say?"

"I suppose so. As long as he won't cost too much. But you must let me pay, or at least contribute. When the house is sold, I'll—"

"We'll sort it out later." William smiled. The prospect of doing something, Celia realized, had at least stopped him worrying about Uncle Ted. "I'll phone him now."

He went into the hall, closing the door behind him. Celia looked down at the letter to Jim. A tiny click made her raise her head. The kitchen door had a spring catch that was slightly out of true with the door frame. It often slipped ajar a few seconds after you thought you had closed it. She could her the dialing of the phone in the hall beyond. She turned back to the letter.

110

. . . that we make a clean break now. I'm sorry it came out so abruptly yesterday. It's not an impulse decision, Jim—I've . . .

"Hallo, Nick? It's William . . ."

The biro froze in Celia's hand. There was something indecently fascinating about hearing one end of other people's telephone conversations.

"No, it's not about Malcolm . . . There's no accounting for taste. . . . Well, I'm not in America and my love life is none of his business. Or yours . . . "

Celia bit her lip and began to write. . . . *been feeling trapped, in need of a change for some time. Please don't take it personally.* She noticed the biro was digging deeper into the paper than before. *In the long run I'm sure it's best for both of us. If I stayed we'd make one another miserable and I'd be a drag on you . . .*

". . . If you've nothing else on, how do you fancy earning some money . . . like twenty pounds an hour, tax free . . . "

Celia threw down the biro and gave up all pretense of not listening. How did William come to have that sort of money to throw around?

"Got some paper? . . . Right, I'm helping a friend who's researching a book on a prewar murder trial. The Landis case. L-A-N-D-I-S. It happened in 1932 near Ely in Cambridgeshire. John Landis was a motor salesman who used arsenic to put down his sister-in-law, Muriel Hinton. We're trying to trace two young relatives, two boys. . . . No, I don't know the Christian names of either. . . . There are reasons why we don't want to advertise. . . . One was born in 1931 . . . the son of John Landis and his wife Beatrice, née Hinton. . . . Yes I know he was a baby at the time. . . . The other was his cousin,

111

the son of Alfred X. Corner, died 1918, and his wife Alexandra, née Hinton, who died the following year. The boy was born after his father died—either 1918 or early 1919. Oh, and there's a strong possibility they may have changed their names. Beatrice died last summer in Luggenhall, Suffolk, and she'd reverted to her maiden name . . ."

Celia continued to listen as William elaborated on and repeated what he had already said. There was no further mention of his love life. As William started to wind up the conversation she picked up her biro again: . . . *I hope to be back next week. I can use the spare room. But in the meantime, I'd appreciate it if—*

She looked up as William returned. "I heard," she said swiftly.

"Good." William smiled. "Saves me repeating everything. Nick said he'd ring when he has some news. In any case I've got to go up to London some time. Work, you know," he added vaguely. "Want some lunch? I could do us an omelette or something."

The telephone rang just as William was adding the egg mixture to the garlic and mushrooms in the pan. Celia ran to answer it. As she had hoped, it was Uncle Ted. She quickly relayed the message from the woman called Lucy. There was a silence at the other end of the line. The omelette sizzled in the kitchen. The smell of garlic drifted out into the hall. *Like arsenic when vaporized.*

"Celia?" said the Major's voice at last. "I'm in Manchester at the moment. I'll come straight back, but I doubt if I'll be home before the early evening. And listen, stay there with William and do nothing, either of you, until we've had a chance to talk. Is that clear. Absolutely *nothing.*"

112

"Absolutely nothing," Celia repeated.

"Good," said Major Dougal. "Good-bye."

"That's all she said? You're absolutely sure?"

William nodded. "She sounded as if she was crying. We were worried."

Major Dougal grunted and swallowed another large mouthful of whisky. He had only got back from Manchester five minutes ago. His first words had been to ask for a drink. That was uncharacteristic—and so was the way he was consuming it like medicine, for the effect rather than for the flavor. Celia had also expected him to comment on the presence of whisky: two years ago, as an economy measure, Uncle Ted had decided not to keep any in the house; William had bought a bottle this afternoon.

"Who was Frederick Forester?" William asked.

"He was two people. Myself and someone else. It doesn't matter—the name was just a convenient fiction to facilitate communication." Major Dougal stared glumly at his empty glass. Celia refilled it.

She blurted out: "Does this tie in with Daddy's death?"

Uncle Ted looked at her over the rim of his glass. His eyes were bloodshot. "In a way, perhaps. Can't be certain. Tell you one thing, though. We've gone as far as we can go. Your father, Corner, the Landis case: there's absolutely no point in looking any further."

"You may feel that but—"

The Major interrupted her: "And I owe you an apology, my dear. It may well be that you were right to be suspicious about Richard's death." He shifted uneasily on the hard kitchen chair. "I know it sounds parodoxical but, having said that, I must now advise you in the strongest

113

possible terms to leave the matter alone. Let the dead lie in peace."

"You'll have to tell us more," said William firmly. For a moment the gazes of father and son were locked together. Celia, sitting between them at the table, thought with surprise: *but how alike they are.*

Uncle Ted was the first to look away. "I knew the man some time ago. You may recall that in my last few years in the army I was detached from regimental duties?"

"I thought you had some sort of staff job."

"Well, yes. Most of the time I was attached to the Ministry of Defense. Flying a desk, as they used to say in the RAF. Terribly dull, most of it. The chap who was the other half of Forester was a sort of colleague. Point is, I asked him about Corner yesterday, and the next thing we know he's . . . well, gone west."

"And you infer a cause-and-effect relationship?" William's words were pedantic; his tone was matter-of-fact. Celia would have welcomed a bit of anger from him, to bolster her own.

"As a rule," replied the Major grimly, "cause and effect is a safer inference than coincidence. And here we have three: my old colleague, Richard, and that old lady in Luggenhall."

Celia slapped the table with the palm of her hand. "Okay, I'm convinced they're not coincidences. I knew that all along. You've just made out a very good case why we should continue. And I will, even if you won't."

"My dear—"

"You can't stop me. It's a free country."

"You don't understand, my dear." Major Dougal frowned. "The Corner court-martial—yes he was; I confirmed that today—and the Landis case are for some rea-

114

son still . . . sensitive as far as someone's concerned. And after what happened to Forester we have to assume that the interested party wields a hell of a lot of clout at M.o.D."

"And isn't afraid of using it," interposed William. "For professional or personal reasons, I wonder?"

"That's irrelevant. The point is, it would be folly for us to take the matter any further. Absolutely suicidal."

"I didn't know people in Whitehall could be so ruthless," said William mildly. "Was murder an established ministry technique when you were there?"

Antagonism crackled like shorting electricity between the two Dougals, despite William's tone of gentle curiosity. Celia took off her glasses and rubbed them vigorously with a paper handkerchief, aware that she did it to indicate her neutrality. The now blurred shoulders of Major Dougal twitched in a shrug.

"My dear William. Part of the price we pay for Celia's free country is the existence of a few official coteries whose conduct can't be judged by ordinary yardsticks. You know that."

"And you were a member of one of them?"

"On the fringes. . . . Sufficiently aware of them to want to keep out of their way. Unless we want to run the risk of being killed ourselves, our only option is a rapid retreat."

Celia argued with Major Dougal for a further twenty minutes. She trimmed the issue down to its essentials; her father's death was an injustice that must offend any fair-minded person; it had to be put right. She found it difficult to appreciate the Major's viewpoint, that fairness was a luxury when one's own survival might be at stake. His cynicism appalled her.

115

William contributed little to the conversation. He stayed on the sidelines, drinking steadily. It suddenly occurred to Celia that he might be in a state of shock: the character of a parent is one of the unstated premises upon which an individual's existence floats; a sudden revision can cause leaks.

Exhaustion and unresolved tension gradually brought the conversation to a halt. The Major's face was tinged with gray.

"I know it's early," he said at last, "but I think I shall have to turn in. But please, will you agree to drop this? For my sake?"

Everyone avoided the others' eyes. There was something indecent in so personal a plea. Celia cleared her throat, embarrassed by her own obstinacy.

There was a slight pressure on her sandaled foot. She glanced up and saw William give a slight shake of his head, followed by a brief but unmistakable wink.

"All right, Uncle Ted," she heard herself saying. "We'll leave it alone. At least for a while."

13

THE FLAT WAS sunk three feet below the level of the pavement. Anyone except an estate agent would call it a basement flat. It was part of the end house of a small terrace, all subdivided into flats, in a cul-de-sac off Shepherd's Bush. The gulleys beside the pavement were deep and lined with leaves and fast-food containers. It was midafternoon and the street was empty. The bustle of traffic around the Green was less than a hundred yards away, but Frangbourne Road had no part in it.

The curtains were drawn across the bay window at the front of the flat. The area it overlooked was a haven for torn newspapers and dented soft drink cans. Access to the flat was by a urine-scented passageway between the house and the high, blank wall of a derelict cinema. The front door had been painted white a long time ago. Before that it had been blue.

William rang the bell. Celia wandered further down the cracked concrete path, past a kitchen window protected by a steel trellis. She paused before a cordon of rubbish which had spewed from an overturned dustbin. There was a small garden beyond, mostly scrubby lawn, which ended in the windowless, red-brick rear of a factory or warehouse. The garden was in shade. It looked as if the sun had only limited access at the best of times.

She turned and said: "Suppose he's not in?"

William pressed the bell again. "I know where there's a spare key. He might have left a message in the flat."

"You'd think he would have phoned by now. It's over three days."

William abandoned the door, slipped past Celia and led the way to the garden. At the back were two more windows, both curtained. A lean-to privy clung to the wall between them. William pushed open its rotting door, revealing a cracked lavatory pan without a seat and a rusted iron cistern thickly coated with spiders' webs. He ran his fingers along the gap between the sagging wooden lintel and the brick course above. With a grunt of satisfaction he pulled out a Yale key.

"Are you sure we should?" Celia asked. "I'm not sure I'd like it in his place."

William shook his head. "Don't worry. I've known him for years—since school, in fact. He likes people dropping in when he's not there. He's not exactly a private person."

With one hand he turned the key; with the other he gave the front door a sharp blow just below the lock.

"Warped," he said, as the door swung backward. "It always sticks." He stopped just inside the door, so abruptly that Celia bumped into him. "Hang on. Look."

She followed his pointing finger and saw a jagged scar of freshly exposed wood on the painted surface of the door frame, about four feet from the ground. William felt down the door and showed her the security chain, still attached to the socket, which should have been in the door frame.

Celia looked around the tiny hall. They were standing on a little pile of mail. A framed poster, advertising the farewell concert of a long-defunct rock band, hung askew on the opposite wall between two partly closed doors. Immediately to their right was a narrow kitchen whose work surfaces and floor were littered with spilt groceries. Heavy-bellied flies and wasps cruised sluggishly over the debris.

"Oh, God," said William softly. He pushed open the left-hand door. Celia followed him into what was evidently the living room. At one end was the bay window toward the street. Books had been pulled from the shelves on either side of the electric fire and left strewn over the carpet. Broken glass crunched beneath William's shoes as he moved forward to examine an electric guitar whose neck had been snapped off. The stripped pine table in the bay was covered with a mound of papers, which had evidently been wrenched from the nearby filing cabinet. Celia's eyes focused on a stray fly, a scout perhaps from the main force in the kitchen, which flew slowly round the room.

William abruptly pushed past Celia into the hall. He nudged open the second door and stopped on the threshold. Celia peered over his shoulder and saw a small bedroom. As in the living room the thin curtains made the light seem subaqueous, without materially affecting visibility. There were flies here as well.

In front of the open wardrobe was a pile of clothes. Beside it was an open doorway, through which Celia could glimpse the corner of a bath. A few feet from where they stood was a double bed, half concealed by the door. More clothes partially obscured a duvet with a floral pattern. She realized with a shock that someone was asleep in bed; she could make out the curved ridge of legs. *Journalists keep irregular hours.* Craning further

119

round the door she glimpsed the naked upper body of a small, swarthy man whose arm was flung up over his face.

Asleep, she thought firmly, *he must be asleep. We shouldn't have—*

William swung round, grasped her by the shoulders and propelled her into the hall. His hands hurt her, momentarily distracting her from the bubble of panic that was threatening to burst out of her.

"Go back to the car," he said, "at once. Lock yourself in. I'll only be a couple of minutes."

She stumbled back to the Deux Chevaux, which they had parked outside the cinema. *Asleep,* she said under her breath as she walked, *he's asleep, he's asleep.* When she reached the car she sat in the passenger seat. She rocked to and fro, repeating those comfortable words again and again.

William's driving at least gave her something else to think about. He drove with complete insensitivity to the limitations of the car and the needs of other drivers. His face was pale and strained, and his shirt was marked with sweat. The route he chose took them on a zigzag course through the inner suburbs of northwest London. He scraped a Cortina in Kensal Rise ("For God's sake, can't they look where they're parking?") and nearly scored a mother-and-pram combo in Brondesbury Park. It occurred to Celia as he parked in a side street between Hampstead Village and the Heath—a welcome relief, well worth the cost of a new cover for the taillight—that he was almost certainly not insured to drive her car.

A pack of children tore down the opposite pavement, whooping in their pursuit of a smaller boy whose blazer and satchel belonged to another era. It was an eerie reminder to Celia of another life and another set of duties. William rolled down the window and lit a cigarette. The shrieking came nearer. The baying of the hunters was overlaid by the higher-pitched keening of their quarry, now face down on the pavement and in imminent danger of losing his short trousers.

"We should do something." About what, even Celia was unsure. Only her misery was certain.

William squinted through the smoke at the fracas outside. "If we rescue him now, he'll only get it worse next time." The cigarette snapped in two between his fingers. He stared blankly at it for an instant before tossing the remains out of the window. "Oh shit," he said softly. "It's my fault Nick was killed."

"It's not. It's mine." Celia saw no reason why William should hog all the guilt. "I—I suppose it couldn't be for some other reason?"

"That would be pushing coincidence too far."

"How did he . . . ?"

"It probably happened last night. The killer must have slipped the Yale, wrenched off the chain and walked straight into the bedroom. It looked as if Nick heard the noise and just had time to sit up. The bullet went in above the right ear. The powder burns suggested close range. Fired from above. Small calibre. Maybe a .22. Even without a silencer it wouldn't have made much noise. Nick must have gone out like a light, which is some consolation."

Which was worse, Celia wondered dully. What had happened? Or the cold, well-informed way in which William had described it?

"We must ring the police," Celia said. "We should have done it at once."

"No," said William flatly. "There's no point."

121

"But we must. It's murder."

"Think it out." William rubbed his nose. "The killer has a high-level M.o.D. connection. He's ruthless and getting more reckless; he didn't even try to make Nick's death look like an accident. We don't know how far his official contacts extend, but they might include the police."

"Oh, come on. You're being paranoid."

"We can't afford to gamble. I gambled with Nick's life. I don't want to gamble with ours. The only thing that keeps us from going the same way as your father and Nick is our anonymity. We'd lose that if we went to the police. And what makes you think they'd believe us? They'd be far more likely to believe we killed Nick ourselves."

The car was a slow oven, fueled by the evening sun. Celia's temper was warming up with the rest of her. She realized that she found more than William's unpalatable words and patronizing tone objectionable. The fundamental unfairness was the real culprit, the Mr. Big of the matter. It was unfair because she was afraid.

Wiliam's argument appalled her, though she recognized its force. Perhaps it was fear that made her see a subtext to his words: *he's scared of the police and it's become axiomatic to avoid them.*

"We might have been seen, going into the flat," she said feebly. "And we must have left fingerprints and things. I'd rather go to the police then have them come to us."

"It's unlikely anyone saw us go in. A calculated risk, and it's worth taking. As for contact traces, I think we're okay. I wiped clean anything we touched. It's not as if we were there for any length of time. And I took the obvious precautions. Look."

122

He dug into his pocket and produced a small, crumpled sheet of paper, which, when smoothed out, proved to have been torn from a loose-leaf notebook.

"Address book," said William with a touch of smugness. "My last five addresses are there."

"You think of everything," Celia said. It wasn't a compliment. "What's that?"

She pointed at the same pocket of William's jeans. A straight rim of gray plastic was visible, peeping above the edge of the pocket. It suddenly and absurdly occurred to Celia that he might think she was pointing to his crotch. She could feel herself beginning to blush.

"A long shot." William pulled out a C90 cassette. "Nick taped a lot of his notes, or thought aloud to a microphone. He'd do it anywhere—in the bath, peeling vegetables." William's voice momentarily faltered. "This cassette was in a little portable machine on the floor by the bed. Whoever went through the flat must have missed it."

Celia took it from him and turned it over. Neither side was labeled. The tape was roughly halfway through a program.

"Turn the ignition key once. We can try it here."

She slotted the cassette into the car's tape deck. Rock music immediately flooded out from the speakers behind them. It was a rough, distorted recording but the medium failed to conceal that the singer was out of tune and that an unhealthy element of competition had gripped the rest of the band.

"My God," William said after the first three bars. "I think I wrote that song." He reached over and snapped off the recording. "Nick wanted to be a pop star when he was fifteen. He never quite grew out of the idea."

He ejected the cassette, flipped it over and reinserted

123

it. A loud rushing noise, not unlike the Niagara Falls on fast-forward, filled the car. It stopped abruptly with a click. The hiss of blank tape followed. William pressed the rewind button. Neither of them spoke. When the tape reached the end, he sat back, groping for a cigarette.

First came a few seconds of hiss, succeeded by a click. This gave way to a long, languorous groan, a sound that expressed sensuous pleasure rather than pain, and which was suddenly terminated by a small, resonant explosion. Another noise—regular but harder to define—followed. A throat was simultaneously and lengthily cleared.

William gave a snort of laughter. "You know what this is? *Krapp's Last Tape* . . . he's on the loo."

"*Um,*" said a dry thin voice. "*Hours so far, twenty-one, call it twenty-five . . . expenses, fifty-six pounds odd, call it sixty. He can afford it. Now, where were we?*"

Another groan, Another, louder explosion.

"*George Henry Landis, born in Cambridge on the ninth of September, 1931. Poor little bugger. Killed during the Blitz in London on the night of the sixteenth/seventeenth of April. Was using the surname Hinton, as was his mother, Mrs. Beatrice Hinton, who reported the death. Mrs. H., described as 'widow,' gave her address as eighteen, King Edward Mansions, Gray's Inn Road, the site of which is now an office block . . .*"

A pause. A third groan, softer and more luxurious. The rustle of paper.

"*. . . Harold John Alfred Corner. He wasn't very difficult. Primary source:* Who's Who. *Born twelfth December, 1918, posthumous son of Alfred X. Corner, who was killed in action earlier the same year. Educated at Stevenage Grammar School and King's College, London . . . In the army during the war but rather reticent about the de-*

124

tails. Which probably means a total lack of glamour or something very cloak-and-dagger. Followed by a long career in the Civil Service, again without many details. He retired a couple of years ago to rest on his laurels, which in this case include a CBE and a CB. Neat but not gaudy. Gives his address as twenty-nine, Consort House, which is a block of service flats just along from the Albert Hall. Oh yes, he married in 1952: Hermione Mary Blacker; they have two daughters . . ."

This time the interlude was longer. The tape hissed to itself. There was a grunt, after which Nick began to hum in a funereal manner. Celia skimmed the tape forwards in short bursts. The humming eventually turned into a long, expressive yawn.

"False alarm, I think." Nick blew his nose and resumed: *"The entry suggested two obvious lines of research. Those flats in Consort House are luxury one bedroom rabbit-hutches for the weekly commuter. The block's an up-market dormitory from Monday night to Thursday night and practically empty for the rest of the time. No room for the wife and kids so, assuming the Corners aren't separated, there has to be another address. The second angle is the Civil Service career; public servants aren't inclined to hide their achievements under a bushel, as a rule. Possible connection with the hint of wartime cloak-and-dagger? I'm beginning to think William's playing me along: there's more here than a prewar murder trial. Worth putting pressure on him?*

"The first line was easy enough to follow. I traced the birth certificates of the Corners' daughters today. Jane Alexandra, born 1959, and Elizabeth Mary, born 1961. The address on the second certificate was the Old Rectory, Reckless, Herts. Stupid name. I looked it up on the map

125

and it's near a village called Nasty. And the Corners are still there. The phone's unlisted, but they're on the voters' list. The younger daughter's at home; Jane Alexandra's flown the nest. As for the second line, it shouldn't be too difficult. Just expensive. I rang Jack and put him on to it. Ten to one he had the answers at the time but he insisted he needed a few days. And he insisted he wouldn't be able to tell me anything unless I took him out to dinner at Biddulph's, which is typical. He's like a camel, that man. Gorges himself as length at someone else's expense and probably exists on crisps for the rest of the time. Mercenary little toad. For some reason it has to be tomorrow night, which meant I had to cancel the band practice. I think I'll charge William double time for unsocial hours and unsocial company. Technically my job's finished as far as William's concerned. I've found Landis and Corner. But I'd swear there's a story here. Something stinks—"

Nick interrupted himself by pulling the chain. His last words were drowned in the flow of water, which was itself curtailed by the click at the end of the recording. Celia switched off the cassette.

"I wonder who put the finger on him." William stared moodily out of the window. The bespectacled little boy had now been deserted by his playmates. The contents of his satchel were scattered along twenty yards of pavement. He was attempting to retrieve his trousers from the sloping roof above a ground floor bay window.

"Biddulph's is a restaurant?" Celia asked.

William nodded. "Also a cocktail bar. It's in Brook Street, just west of New Bond Street. I had a drink there once. It's quite new and very expensive. Desperately trying to pretend it's chic." He stopped and, in a quite different tone, added: "Oh, shit. I won't be a moment."

126

He got out of the car and walked along to the diminutive front garden overlooked by the bay window. As Celia watched, he conferred briefly with the boy, hoisted himself up on the low window sill and yanked the trousers from the roof. The boy hastily put them on. William acted on an apologetic mime, which, Celia eventually realized, must be for the benefit of an unseen but understandably agitated householder.

William's altruism gave her amusement, mixed with a dash of relief; it was a welcome antidote to the effect his cool-headed response to Nick's death had had on her. But her attention was partly elsewhere, exploring a hypothesis that had suddenly suggested itself to her.

"Priggish little beast," William said without animosity as he got back into the car. "Did you see? I tried to bring a little sunshine into his life by offering him a quid. He spurned it. Said he'd been warned about strangers like me."

"There's no justice," Celia said, as lightly as she could manage. She privately qualified the remark: there was only the justice you made for yourself.

"We'd better go home." William ejected the tape and tapped it thoughtfully with a fingernail. "It's about time we started taking my father's advice. Do you want to drive?"

"Yes. But I'm not going, yet. I'll drop you off at Liverpool Street and you can get a train."

14

"**M**Y NAME IS MARSTON," William said firmly. "Nicholas Marston."

The headwaiter, a plump, tail-coated individual with a round white face, allowed his gaze to travel slowly down from the absence of tie around William's neck to the faded jeans on his lower half. William slowly drew a five-pound note from his pocket and glanced at it with a slight frown, as if uncertain what it was doing there.

"I booked a table for three at eight."

"Of course, sir." The headwaiter, clearly anxious to add a personal touch, added: "You rang this evening to confirm the booking. Originally for two, but now for three?"

"That's right." The note slithered through William's fingers and slipped unobtrusively into the headwaiter's hand. "We'd like a quiet drink beforehand." There was the slightest of stresses on the adjective. "Oh, and when my guest arrives, would you bring him over?"

"Yes, sir. Would the booth at the end be suitable?"

The cocktail bar at Biddulph's had been designed by someone with a fondness for stables. Each table was separated from its neighbors by a four-foot-high partition of

128

dark-stained wood. Perhaps it was appropriate, Celia thought: from behind one of the partitions came the unmistakable neigh of a Sloane Ranger in a skittish, Friday night mood.

The headwaiter ushered Celia and William to the stall at the end. Its narrow, rectangular table was made of shiny imitation oak and flanked by two forbiddingly austere benches. A small vase held three white rosebuds made of cloth and plastic.

The headwaiter produced a reserved notice for their table. "We may get a little crowded later on, sir," he murmured. He bowed Celia into her seat. Another waiter appeared with little dishes of nuts, savory biscuits and olives. "Gerald will look after you, sir." The words were addressed to William but intended for Gerald.

Celia and William sat in silence while Gerald fetched their drinks. Celia was grateful that William had insisted on coming. But she wished she had been able to wear something more suited to the occasion. Her dress was badly rumpled after a day spent mainly in the car; and even when ironed it was not what you would choose to wear when dining at a place with the pretensions of Biddulph's. She would have given a lot to have been able to wash her hair and have a shower. William had a flat in West Hampstead and she had suggested that they go there before coming on to Biddulph's; in any case she was curious to see how he lived. His refusal had disconcerted her, and the memory of it tempered her gratitude toward him with irritation.

That was one reason for the silence between them. The other was that it was difficult to make light conversation when the evening ahead was so uncertain. Would Jack come? Could he be persuaded to talk to them? Would he have anything of interest to say? Would seeing him be tantamount to signing their own death warrants?

She sipped her orange juice—at least it was fresh here—and glanced at William, who was looking with profound interest into his slender glass of Black Velvet. He lifted his eyes.

"You look beautiful," he said. "I wish— Chin up. Here comes Mr. Toad."

The headwaiter materialized with a squat little man in tow. William slid swiftly from the bench and stood close to their guest with his hand held out. It was a nicely judged maneuver, since the headwaiter was close behind Jack; it would be difficult for him to retire without awkwardness. *Toad sandwich*, thought Celia, and felt a bewilderingly contradictory urge to giggle and faint at the same time.

"Jack!" William grabbed the man's hand and pumped it vigorously. "Nick's on his way—been delayed. He wanted us to meet. Oh, I'm another Nicholas by the way, and this is . . . Maggie. Let me get you a drink."

Celia reached up and, with precision timing, seized the hand just as William released it. It was faintly clammy; and there was no reciprocal movement when she gripped it.

"Nick's delayed?" Jack's voice lacked intonation; each syllable bore the same uniform rasp; it might have been produced by a rather primitive microelectronic chip.

"He rang me from Shepherd's Bush just before we came here. Something about a blocked drain." William consulted his watch. "He shouldn't be more than ten minutes. What can I get you?"

"I'll have a Manhattan," said Jack promptly. "A large one." He spoke to the headwaiter who, with a disdainful

130

jerk of his head, tossed the order on to the hovering Gerald. Celia got the impression that the five pounds worth of goodwill was fast running out.

Jack showed signs of wanting to sit by Celia. William adroitly and wordlessly herded him on to the opposite bench and sat down beside him, blocking any move to escape.

Though small, Jack looked too corpulent to be light on his feet. Celia judged he was a little older than William. He had a shock of wiry hair and gray, sagging jowls. It was a fried-food complexion. Where the fat was heavy, particularly under the jawline, there sprouted little clumps of black stubble that had escaped the razor. His muddy brown eyes bulged slightly and moved restlessly. He had a nervous tic, which involved the mastication of invisible food. It must be invisible, otherwise you would see it; Jack was not the sort to close his mouth while eating.

His clothes were calculatedly eccentric and not very clean. A green deerstalker lay on the table between them. He wore a tweed jacket whose shoulders and elbows were decorated with superfluous leather patches. It had a great many pockets, sewn on to the outside of the cloth. Beneath the jacket was a check shirt with a grubby collar, a striped tie, and a yellow waistcoat. A steel watchchain stretched across a belly that could legitimately be called a corporation. Celia was glad his underclothes were not available for inspection.

The Manhattan arrived. Jack swallowed it in two mouthfuls. William signaled for another and pushed the appetizers toward him. The thick fingers with their cracked nails quarried through the little dishes.

At least they had cleared the first hurdle: Jack had

131

come—which meant he couldn't have heard of Nick's death—and he didn't seem unduly disturbed. She wondered what he did for a living. He lacked the polish of a professional gossip-gatherer. More likely he was a minor functionary in some branch of the civil service. But, if that were the case, you wouldn't have expected him to have access to information about Corner.

"We might as well begin," said William. He had to raise his voice to be heard above the crunching of biscuits. "There's no need to wait for Nick."

"I don't agree. I don't know who you are. You can buy me a drink if you want but I don't have to talk to you."

"Let me explain," said William softly. "We hired Nick to do some research. Part of that made it necessary for him to hire you. In Nick's absence—"

"Correction. Nick hasn't hired me. Yet. That's the first thing on my agenda." Jack drained his cocktail and looked expectantly for Gerald.

"There's no problem. We want some information. If you've got it, we'll pay for it. Now."

"Two hundred quid in used notes," Jack said flatly. "No consecutive serial numbers. Prepaid, of course."

William was reaching inside his jacket when Celia interrupted. "We'll pay in two installments. Before and after." She felt annoyed with both men for leaving her out of the conversation. "And first, we'll need some indication that you have what we want."

Jack's eyes bulged in her direction, noting her properly for the first time. There was no visible change in him, but Celia received the impression that for some reason he was pleased. *He likes to bargain,* Celia thought. *He's used to sitting round a negotiating table.* The thought coalesced into a question: *Union?* A senior union official,

132

however low his rank in the civil service hierarchy, might have access to a wide range of information. He might be prepared to sell some of it for ideological as well as financial reasons. Nick's political sympathies, Celia recalled William saying, had been considerably left of center.

"You want to know about a man called Harold Corner. Maggie, isn't it?" Jack stopped as Gerald set down his third Manhattan on the table. Neither of the others had touched their drinks since his arrival. "A lot of people want to know about Harold. I wonder who you're with."

"Freelance," said William.

Jack sniggered. "Pull the other one."

"Does it matter?" Celia asked. "A hundred down and another hundred after you've told us?"

"Okay," Jack leered toward her. "Anything to oblige a lady with such a pretty name."

William extracted an obscenely large bundle of notes from his pocket. He laid some of them on the bench between himself and Jack. Jack's thick lips moved as he silently counted them. He stuffed the pile into an inner pocket of his waistcoat.

Suddenly he stood up. "I'll just phone Nick. Like to be sure we're all on the level."

William's hand shot up and grabbed the little finger of Jack's left hand. The dull eyes sharpened with pain. "I'd sit down," suggested William. "We're in a bit of a hurry."

It was neatly done. The snippet of controlled violence suggested an unknown but significant quantity in reserve. William's tone hinted at an assurance that Celia hoped he didn't feel. It was nothing but bluff, of course. If Jack chose to make a scene he would walk out with a hundred pounds and no risk of reprisals.

But he didn't. He sunk back on to the bench, massaging

133

his little finger. Purely physical aggression was alien to him. There were beads of sweat on his forehead. He clutched his drink.

"Nick will soon be here," said William soothingly. "So will your other hundred, once you've told us about Corner." He slipped a hand inside his tweed jacket and edged an inch toward Jack. Jack jerked away, spilling a few drops of his drink on his lap.

"There's not much to know." Jack sounded apologetic. "And a lot of what I've got is just rumor. They say he worked for the Special Operations Executive in the war. Not in the field: he was one of the Baker Street boys. His war was mainly interdepartmental. When he was demobbed he joined the Civil Service. Home Office." Jack scooped up the last olive. "Funny, really. People with an SOE background generally chose M.o.D. or the Foreign Office, or maybe one of those dependent organizations we're not supposed to know about."

"What did he actually do?" Celia asked.

"Not much at the Home Office, that's for sure. He was in the establishment right up to his retirement. But in fact he spent over thirty years on one committee. It's had a lot of names—Interdepartmental Administrative Liaison is the current label. Corner started in the rank and file of the secretariat and ended up vice-chairman. Even now he's retained on some sort of advisory basis."

Jack leant back against the wall and swallowed the last of his Manhattan. He had the slightly smug expression of a person who knows he has earned his money.

Celia wanted to kick him. Instead she said, as casually as she could manage: "What exactly does the committee do?"

"It was one of the innovations of the Attlee Govern-

134

ment. Its function is to coordinate the activities of certain sections of the Home Office, the FCO, and M.o.D. The dirty ones. IALC's job is to avoid the sort of cock-ups they had in the war—you now, like when SIS were always treading on SOE's toes, accidentally on purpose, I shouldn't be surprised, and vice versa. If an employee of HMG isn't allowed to belong to a union, it's a safe bet his work is monitored by IALC."

"And who does the committee report to?" asked William.

"Cabinet Secretary. In crisis situations direct to the PM."

"You've not told us much about Corner," said Celia suddenly. "Not two hundred pounds' worth."

Jack shrugged. Some of his self-confidence had oozed back while he was talking. "There's not a lot to say about him. On IALC, keeping a low profile is part of the job. You'd have expected someone of his seniority and length of service to get a knighthood. Maybe that means he offended someone a little higher up the ladder. It's dog eat dog with that lot. What can you expect with a system that encourages these self-perpetuating ruling cliques. If I had my way—"

"Have another drink," William said. "Waiter!"

When Gerald brought the fourth Manhattan, William stood up. He dropped a twenty-pound note on the waiter's tray and told him to keep the change.

Jack said: "Aren't we eating here? Nick said—"

Celia picked up her handbag and got up. "Why don't you wait for him?"

William dropped five more twenties on the bench. "Good-bye."

On the pavement outside Biddulph's William hailed a

taxi. As it waited to make a U-turn, Celia asked, "Why were you in such a hurry to leave?"

"He was beginning to think we were harmless. We don't want him trying to extract another installment. I just hope he's harmless too."

Harmless? Celia thought, as the taxi whisked them north to the side street in St. John's Wood, where they had left her car. The only harmless person she had met in the last fortnight was herself. And that included the two Dougals.

15

MAJOR DOUGAL HAD been on intimate and even comfortable terms with his mind for over half a century. It therefore came as something of a shock to him when he gradually realized that stress had surreptitiously altered it. His old familiar mind had been replaced with two new ones, using the components of their predecessor.

It reminded him of a very long express train whose carriages, toward the end of the journey, were divided into two, each traveling along its own lines to a destination that bore no relation to the other's.

One of these new minds operated in the clear light of day. It belonged to the Major Dougal who was trying to live his normal life. It blocked out the memories of cavorting with dragons. In particular it blocked out those three disturbing and inexplicable events—the deaths of Richard Prentisse and Mrs. Landis, and the removal of Colonel Blaines. Further investigation could only be harmful. Therefore it was best to pretend that the events had never happened. He was aware that any pretense or fiction, if lived and believed for long enough, would eventually become fact.

The other mind was a creature of darkness. It operated like a skirmisher behind the enemy lines, on the frontier between sleeping and waking. It slipped like a saboteur into his dreams. It drew secret strength from the knowledge of the past and the fears of the present.

The second mind—so much more devious than the first—worked insidiously on his fears for William and Celia. On Tuesday night they had undertaken to let the matter drop, under considerable pressure from himself. He had believed them at the time; but now he wondered whether he had merely believed what he wanted to hear. Old training had resurfaced in the last few days, and that training included the ability to evaluate facts dispassionately. He suspected that the objective assessor he had once been would have placed little or no reliance on what they said on Tuesday night. The objective assessor would argue that William and Celia were operating under emotional duress: they had agreed with him to prevent him worrying. The assessor would emphasize that Celia in her own way was just as headstrong as her father had been. And William—

William was an unknown quantity.

The other strength of this second mind could be ascribed to the insatiable demands of his own curiosity. He *wanted* to know why Richard had died, why Corner's file was so sensitive, and how the court-martial and the Landis case were linked. He hungered for the answers for their own sake, not because he had any particular use for them. As he had felt so often in the past, justice and vengeance were both abstractions; only knowledge was real. Even if he had wanted justice, he accepted that in this case it was impossible.

For three days the facts that he and the others had gathered floated in his second mind; and nothing he could do would sink them. They eddied ceaselessly, combining,

138

fragmenting, and recombining. None of the patterns made sense. Too many pieces were missing.

On Friday the eddies grew more violent and harder to ignore. The reason for this was that William and Celia had gone to London. They had publicized their reasons for going to suspicious detail: William was going to an auction at Christie's where there was some Lowestoft china, which he had a professional interest in; Celia wanted to do some shopping; and they planned to go to the theatre afterwards.

Much against his will the Major wondered what they were really doing. At one point he picked up the phone to ring Christie's just to see if there was a china sale on today. He stopped just in time, suddenly revolted by the idea of spying on his own son.

By the afternoon, Major Dougal was frankly jittery. If he refused to let himself worry about William and Celia, some other aspect of the business popped in his mind.

One of them was Colonel Blaines. *Gone West on the District Line. . . .* The Major had allowed Celia and William to infer from this and from Lucy's tears that the man she called Forester was dead. But Fang was alive; and in some ways that was more unfortunate for him. Major Dougal had wanted them to misunderstand for two reasons—he hoped another death might be more effective than the truth in frightening them off, for their own good; and the obscure loyalty that still bound him to his old firm made him unwilling to explain to outsiders the niceties of in-house slang, even if the slang was now out of date.

The London Underground lines provided a convenient range of metaphors for private conversations in public places. If someone went west on the Piccadilly Line, for example, it meant he or she had gone to Heathrow, and hence was abroad. To say a person was on the Circle Line now meant he was in London on a permanent basis, and no longer likely to be posted elsewhere. The District Line for some reason had particularly unfortunate connotations. To go east on it implied your destination was more likely to be Moscow than Upminster, and that you were traveling on the same sort of one-way ticket as Messrs. Burgess and Philby.

To go west on the District Line did not mean you were dead—that distinction was reserved for the Northern Line going south. On the contrary, it signified you were alive and kicking against the pricks in that farm on the South Wales border.

The farm was Her Majesty's deep freeze; it was reserved for those of her servants whose loyalty or efficiency had suddenly become suspect. It was an official limbo where you could wait indefinitely, pending judgment.

No one died at the farm—it wasn't that sort of place. A few of its guests eventually returned to their old jobs, their careers in no way hampered by the experience. More of them—perhaps the majority—were transferred to new posts, usually on the same salary and with the same pension rights; but fewer files than before came across their desks and their colleagues were wary of them, as if they might be tainted with some kind of moral leprosy. The third—and by far the smallest—group among the farm's guests went on to appear at the Old Bailey.

All categories of guests had one thing in common when they left the farm: their pasts and their presents were now incapable of concealment. They were transparent people.

140

The Major tried to remember which branch of the inquisition administered the farm. He fancied it was one of those interdepartmental committees that lurked in the shade of the Official Secrets Act, whose powers could be assumed to range over the entire security/intelligence-gathering spectrum.

It was difficult to believe that an emergency session of deep vetting would distill anything treasonable from Blaines's life—though one could never be sure. The truth about anyone's past wasn't immutable; it was at the mercy of the person who was interpreting it. Look what happened to poor Roger Hollis. Even if Blaines got back his old job at the end of it, his reputation would never be quite the same.

The Major shivered. If Lucy hadn't turned the risk of warning him, swayed by some obscure loyalty of her own, he himself might have ended up at the farm. Sooner or later he would have tried to get in touch with Fang. As far as the Official Secrets Act was concerned you were never retired.

What else was there? It confirmed what he had already known—that someone with a great deal of influence among the dragons was behind this business.

But *why?*

Major Dougal realized with a start that the evening had crept up on him unnoticed. The colors of the sitting room had faded; there were shadows in the corner; and the glass of the windows had turned a dull yellow from the streetlamps outside. He glanced at his watch: nearly eight o'clock. He pushed away the heap of fruitless speculations and tried to persuade himself he was hungry.

He failed. He had always found it difficult to work up an appetite when he was worried. But a drink was an-

141

other matter—and there was still some of William's whisky left.

In the kitchen he poured himself a couple of fingers and added the same amount of water. He returned to the sitting room, switched on the lights and drew the curtains. The room became vividly normal again, and Major Dougal tried to follow its example. He was often alone on Friday nights: what did he usually do with them?

There was that article he was meant to be writing on the cavalry tactics of Prince Rupert of the Rhine, but he knew he wouldn't be able to concentrate on serious work. He picked up the *Telegraph* and thumbed through the paper until he reached the television programs. In a few minutes the penultimate episode of a serial about the intrigues of bankers, industrialists, and their extremely complicated families would be on. The title was familiar: surely William and Celia had mentioned watching it?

He switched on the television and sank back in his chair. On the black-and-white screen two singers, arm in arm and swaying gently from side to side, explained in quite unnecessary detail why they were so happy to be together; as they crooned they smiled impartially at each other and the camera. Major Dougal read the obituaries until the stirring theme music of the serial warned him that it was safe to look up. He stared curiously at the shots behind the titles. These showed the chief characters of the serial taking an innocent pleasure in the good life that was their birthright. The good life in this case largely consisted of bottles of champagne, stacks of bank notes, roulette wheels, and the low-cut evening gowns that were *de rigueur* for the female members of the cast at all times of the day.

The music subsided, and Major Dougal leaned forward.

142

They were in a gigantic room, which was evidently designed to be a gentleman's library. It was furnished in a way that few gentlemen could now afford, or would have chosen if they could, particularly if they actually read books. A venerable old man in a white tuxedo set down what must have been half a pint of brandy on the marble mantelpiece.

"I swear to God, Marty," he remarked in a gravely midwestern accent, "if you harm a hair on my granddaughter's head, you can kiss that Federal contract goodbye."

"Damn you, Julius." The camera panned to a younger man with a dark, pencil-thin moustache, who was also in some sort of evening dress. Just to make his feelings on the subject quite clear, he added: "Damn you to hell."

The scene changed to the exterior of a large and vaguely Georgian mansion whose facade was dominated by an enormous portico. The elderly gentleman stood at the front door, vigorously shaking his fist. The younger man, mouthing silent curses, leapt behind the wheel of a white Rolls Royce Corniche and departed down the drive so quickly and so noisily that one could only assume that supernatural agencies were at work.

Julius slumped against one of the white pillars that conveniently clustered around the door. He clutched his heart. His face twisted like a man with indigestion. He was naturally concerned about his granddaughter, the Major realized. There were footsteps clicking across the hall. Julius looked up, showing the camera a profile of ravaged nobility. A dark, beautiful girl with sucked-in cheeks and an immaculate cloud of black hair stood framed in the doorway. She wore a long black dress, which was slit in four strategically sited places.

"Ju?" she whispered huskily. "I've done it. You wanna see it?"

Julius extended his hand imperiously. She gave him a sheet of paper, which he studied with care. He then transferred his attention to the girl's cleavage. "It might work," he said thoughtfully. "The shareholders would force the Third International to accept the bid if they knew their chief executive was . . . " His voice died away and he looked up sharply at the girl's face. "Christabel, you're sure there's no copy of this?" he demanded curtly. "No way it can be traced back? You must have used one of the electronics. I hope you've put the cassette ribbon and the daisy wheel on the furnace. We can't be too careful."

The camera left them in the middle of their deliberations and returned to Marty and his Corniche. Major Dougal followed Marty into the casino, ignoring a stab of guilt that assailed him on the way: he really should be working on Prince Rupert.

But you are working. The Major's second mind emerged from its cerebral recess with an idea in tow. *Think about it,* suggested the second mind, as seductively as a disembodied Christabel.

Major Dougal twitched in his chair in a physical attempt to shrug off the siren. He concentrated on the screen. This nonsense could evidently entertain two reasonably intelligent people like William and Celia. Perhaps he was missing something. The telephone rang. For an instant he tried to ignore it, willing himself to remain in the security of this American fairyland. Then the thought that it might be William brought him to his feet. He answered the phone on the third ring.

"Ted, is that you? It's Margaret Prentisse here."

144

"Hullo, Margaret." The Major pulled the door of the sitting room toward him, shutting off the sound of the television. "What can I do for you?"

"Is Celia with you?" Margaret sounded different, the Major noted automatically. She was speaking faster and less precisely than usual.

"No, I'm afraid not." He considered adding that she was probably with William in a London theatre at this moment but decided not to; that was Celia's business.

"I'm worried," Margaret burst out. "The electricity has gone. I suppose it's a fuse. Richard used to do that sort of thing. Or Celia if he wasn't around. So I thought if she was with you . . . "

Major Dougal suddenly remembered a conversation he had with Richard. It must have been years ago. They had been talking about phobias for some reason. *Funny thing about 'em,* Richard had said as the barriers went down with the third glass of brandy, *is that they seem to affect the least likely people sometimes. Take Margaret for instance. If a squadron of panzers had rolled up to the house, she wouldn't have been scared. She'd probably have sued Hitler for ruining her lawn. But leave her alone in the dark and she's terrified . . .*

"I expect she's out with William," Margaret continued. "She might have phoned." There was an edge of hysteria in her voice.

The Major mumbled sympathetically into the phone and thought with yearning of what was going on in the sitting room. The serial seemed far more alluring than it had done a few seconds ago. But his sense of duty didn't waver. He was of a generation whose chivalry was no less genuine for being automatic. And Margaret, as Richard's widow, had a double claim on him.

145

"Would it help if I came over?" he offered with all the warmth he could manage. "I'm all right at the simpler do-it-yourself things. I could bring a screwdriver and some fuse wire." A sudden inspiration made him add: "And a couple of torches, of course."

There was no doubt about Margaret's relief. She almost purred with cordiality. She assured him that she would collect him in the car *in two shakes of a lamb's tail* and rang off.

Major Dougal snapped off the television and went into the garage with a carrier bag to collect the tools he might need. On his way he passed the old coal bunker, which, since the installation of the gas central heating, had served to house a rusting watering can and a pile of seed trays. He flashed his torch over it and thought of Julius's mansion with its convenient furnace.

Once she arrived, Margaret found it difficult to stop talking. As she drove them back to her house she explained at length what had happened. The evening was chilly, and for the first time in several months she had switched on a little portable electric fire. It seemed a quicker and less expensive solution than turning on the entire central heating system. Of course she could have lit a real fire, but they never seemed to burn properly for her. As soon as she had switched on the fire, there was a *bang!* and all the electricity failed—lights, television, fridge, and all. There was a torch by her bedside, but in her hurry she had dropped it, breaking the bulb. There were candles, she was sure, in one of the kitchen cupboards, though she hadn't actually seen them for months. In the dark she couldn't find them in their usual place. She hinted accusingly that Mrs. Gann must have put them somewhere else when she last did out the cupboards.

146

Major Dougal listened with half an ear. When they reached the house she followed him closely, holding one of the torches and still talking. He found the electricity meter and the fuse box in the cupboard under the stairs. It was hardly surprising that something had gone wrong. The wiring here was a hodge-podge: in the past thirty years bits had been added and subtracted until the result was a dangerously living musuem of electrical archaeology. Richard had been meaning to have it rewired for the last ten years.

The trouble wasn't hard to find. The trip switch was down—the source of Margaret's *bang*. He checked the fuses one by one. There were two for the wall sockets and one of them had blown. He pulled it out and flicked up the trip switch. Lights came on all over the house.

Behind him, Margaret screwed up her eyes and let out a long breath. She saw that the torch in her hand was still shining; she snapped it off. Her face was grimy and her hair was in a mess, but the old fighting spirit was back.

"*Well!* Is that all?" She sounded almost disappointed.

"Not quite." The Major unscrewed both ends of the fuses and shook out the blackened fragments of wire into the palm of his hand. "It looks like three-amp wire in there—you really needed thirteen. Switching on the electric fire probably overloaded it. And when that happened the trip switch automatically cut off all the power, for safety's sake."

"Didn't make me feel safe," said Margaret trenchantly.

"I'll put some more fuse wire in here." The Major's voice was patient. "Then I'd better check the time switch for your hot water, and have a look at the fire itself."

Margaret patted her hair. Her fingertips acted as her eyes: she knew she wasn't looking her best. She edged into the hall. "Would you like some tea?"

147

"Please." The Major snipped off the appropriate length of new wire and inserted it in the fuse holder. "By the way, where's the electric fire?"

There was an infinitesimal pause—just long enough for the Major to notice it and, glancing at Margaret, to see her eyes sliding away from his.

"It's in the study. I unplugged it before I came out. I'll just put the kettle on."

Major Dougal returned to his work. Margaret had a perfect right to be in the study, though in the last few weeks she had made a point of leaving the clearing up in there to Celia. It was only strange that she had hesitated before admitting to it.

He replaced the mended fuse and checked the time switch for the water. The clatter of crockery came through from the kitchen. The Major quickly and quietly climbed the stairs and opened the study door.

The room was almost exactly how it had been when he had seen it last. The only difference was a little pile of torn paper and cardboard, which was heaped like a sacrificial offering in front of the electric fire. He squatted beside the pile and poked through its contents.

Someone had systematically devastated copies of Richard Prentisse's three most recent books.

16

I T WAS THE wanton savagery of the act that surprised him most. Covers of the books had been folded and stamped on. Many of the pages had been torn in four. A book was not an easy thing to destroy. To do so like this required endurance and determination. It was irrational, of course. Nothing could have been concealed within the books that would only yield to this sort of treatment.

One of the covers showed the heel marks clearly. There was no doubt about it: a woman's shoe had done the damage.

Margaret must have known he would find this—yet she had made no attempt to stop him. He had to go and find her.

But first there was another job to do. Major Dougal glanced over his shoulder. The landing was empty. He left the door ajar and crossed to the table between the windows. The typewriter, an old IBM, was still there. He looked closely at what he could see of the ribbon. It was dark brown and shiny—the sort which was usable only once; he was over the first hurdle. To the right it was blank. To the left he could just make out the letters *urs faithfully*.

The Major wasted a precious moment trying to find the

149

catch that released the cover. In the end he found there were two, carefully concealed under the typewriter. The cover swung up and back. He disengaged both spools and removed the whole ribbon from the typewriter. His clumsiness and ignorance made it a far messier business than he had anticipated. The ribbon was over three-quarters used: with luck he was over the second hurdle. He wrapped it in his handkerchief and stuffed it in his jacket pocket.

He would have liked to insert a new ribbon—it was always a good policy to leave things as they were—but he had no idea where they were kept, and he doubted his ability to handle the technology involved, even if he managed to find a spare.

"Tee-ee!" Margaret's voice fluted up the stairs. It sounded totally normal. Major Dougal hastily returned to the landing and said he would be down as soon as he had washed his hands.

Margaret was sitting at the kitchen table. As soon as he appeared, she poured his tea.

"All serene." The Major loathed the fake joviality he could hear in his voice. "But it might be an idea to get a qualified electrician round to have a look at the wiring. Some of it looks pretty dicey."

He sat down and took a sip of his tea. In the interval Margaret had repaired the ravages to her face and hair and was back to her usual painted perfection. Her eyes were bright; they followed the movements of his cup with the involuntary abruptness of a startled bird.

"Are you all right?" The Major cleared his throat. "What I mean is . . . is there anything else I can do while I'm here?"

Margaret huddled forward, her elbows on the table

150

and her chin resting on her hands. "I'm worried," she said harshly. "Not just about what they're doing now—though Celia might have phoned, don't you think? But the whole business: where will it all lead? I don't want to rake up the past," she said, meaning the reverse, "but we have to face it: those two aren't good for one another."

"They're grown up now." He watched her mouth tighten. "Even if we could interfere, which I doubt, I don't think we should." The words were fatuous, he knew. Margaret wasn't really worried about the children. There was also a certain irony in what he had said: if he could interfere to keep William and Celia away from the dragons, he would. "Should" be damned.

Margaret stared intently at him. "Don't take this personally, Ted. But just *look* what's been happening since William came back. Celia's broken her engagement. Richard was very fond of Jim, and so am I. She's thrown up a very promising career—and probably damaged Jim's by the impetuous way she chose to do it. She's selling her share in the cottage, which is the one investment she's got. It's completely irresponsible and selfish. Richard would have been dreadfully upset. In a way it's a blessing . . . " Margaret sipped daintily at her tea. Her hand was shaking and some of the tea slopped into the gay circle of flowers on the saucer.

"I wonder if Richard's death has made her want to reassess her life," Major Dougal suggested gently. "The death of a parent can be very traumatic." *And so can the death of your husband—or your wife.* "Perhaps all we can do is be on hand if she needs us."

He stopped when he saw the effect his homespun parental guidance was having. Tears, streaked with makeup, were trickling silently down Margaret Pren-

151

tisse's cheeks. *Not all china dolls are stuffed with sawdust.* He should have realized what she was going through. She and Richard had had a good marriage, however it might have appeared to outsiders. He had been stupid enough to believe that her grief was as superficial as her face. He had seen the same thing happen with soldiers. They could suffer the most horrible experiences and seem unchanged by them. Then—in a few days or a few weeks—the dam would crack and the reaction poured out in a torrent.

Understanding did not lead to action. Major Dougal feared the power of a weeping woman. He rapidly and ignobly reviewed the traditional remedies. The offer of his handkerchief was out from the start. He'd noticed paper handkerchiefs in the bathroom, but to dash out of the kitchen at this juncture would seem callous. A consoling embrace would be a difficult maneuver to accomplish in their physical circumstances, and would probably fail to comfort her. Only Richard Prentisse could do that.

Finally he said, "Oh my dear," in a voice which he hoped would sound both sympathetic and bracing. It seemed to work. Margaret sniffed twice and reached up her sleeve for a pale blue handkerchief.

"I know it's silly," she said with a trace of her former briskness. "The electricity going off was the final straw. Alone in the darkness."

"We need a drink," the Major said gruffly. "Shall I get us some brandy? It's in the dining room, isn't it?"

Margaret nodded and he slipped out of the kitchen. She needed a moment to catch her breath and find a mirror. He needed a glass of brandy.

When he returned with the glasses in one hand and the

152

bottle in the other, she was calm again. He poured for both of them and pushed her glass across the table.

"I saw the books upstairs." It had to be said sooner or later, and he wanted to get it over. "It was you?"

She nodded again. She held her glass in both hands and took a deep swallow. The spirit made her cough. It said a lot about her state of mind that she didn't bother to cover her mouth with her hand. Between coughs she said, "So ... alone ... "

"I know." Major Dougal absently rotated the ring on his little finger. "It will get easier, you know."

"I could *kill* him," Margaret said with passionate illogic. Her hand knocked over her glass; the Major caught it before it rolled off the table. "I could just about bear it if he had died in any other way. But killing himself was like slapping my face."

"So you took your revenge on his books?"

"He loved them. You know that." Margaret rubbed her eyes. "It would have been different if I could have given him children." She reached for the bottle and refilled her glass. "When the lights went off, I almost thought it was ... "

Her voice died away but Major Dougal could complete the sentence. *Richard taking his revenge from beyond the grave.*

"That's absolutely ridiculous, Margaret. You were more important to him than anything, or anyone."

"Was I?" Margaret's eyes were bleak. "Then why did he kill himself? Why didn't he leave a message? You should know. You were his friend." She made it sound like a crime.

To tell the truth would have been so easy: *It's almost certain that Richard was murdered. He loved you. He*

153

didn't leave you of his own free will. But it would be fatal, perhaps literally, to give Margaret a hint of the truth. It might bring her a little consolation; but her inevitable efforts to get justice would wreck her life and probably his and Celia's as well. He said:

"I think he had some sort of a brainstorm. Something irrational trapped his mind." He groped for bromide. "For a few hours he wasn't himself. But you mustn't think it invalidates the rest of his life, and how he thought about you. It would be exactly the same if he had gone senile and become a vegetable for the last years of his life. It wouldn't destroy or betray what had gone before. You must see that."

"I suppose so," said Maragaret drearily. Her hostess manner briefly returned. "You've been very kind, Ted. I think I might take a sleeping pill and go to bed."

"I could always stay until Celia gets back." He added hastily, "Downstairs, I mean."

Margaret declined. She had reached a watershed, Major Dougal thought, and it was unlikely that anyone but herself could help her over it. She wouldn't harm herself—she was no more suicidal by nature than Richard.

He refused her offer to ring for a taxi—he preferred to walk home. She came to see him out. On the doorstep he surprised them both by asking if he could take her out to dinner one night next week. She surprised them both by accepting.

It was Friday night, but the streets of Plumford were nearly empty, apart from bursts of activity around the pubs in Market Street. The Major walked quickly, hardly aware of his surroundings. Seeing Margaret like that made him feel he had failed Richard; he was angry with himself.

154

As Margaret moved away from center stage his worries about William and Celia returned. In the pocket of his tweed jacket the typewriter ribbon bounced lightly against his hip. The windows of the bungalow were dark. Major Dougal paused at the gate. It was absurd to be paranoid. He could only be at risk if Blaines had talked. He tried to put himself in Fang's place. If the people at the farm asked him why he had asked to see Corner's file, he could perfectly reasonably attribute it to a routine check on recently computerized files. After all, spot checks on the standard of record-keeping were part of the Colonel's brief. He wouldn't want to mention Major Dougal because the whole business smacked of private enterprise financed from the petty cash. Few things could upset the dragons more than that. Unless the farm's methods had changed in the last few years, no one would employ sodium pentothal, or one of the cruder forms of torture, on the guests: it was not the farm's style—for the guests, whether guilty or innocent, were too important to take liberties with.

Nevertheless Major Dougal paused. It felt childish, but he dredged up the old routine. After a few seconds he walked on up the road to the pillar-box, where he pretended to post a letter. On the way there and back he scanned the houses on either side and paid particular attention to parked cars that he hadn't seen before.

Nothing was abnormal.

He opened the gate and walked quietly round the bungalow, keeping to the shadows of the garden. A cat crossed his path, staring contemptuously up at him. Its eyes bounced back the yellow of the streetlamps. *How pathetically childish*, they seemed to say. *What do you think you're doing on my territory?*

The Major wiped his forehead—the cat had taken him

155

by surprise—and let himself in at the back door. The familiar emptiness of the house briefly overwhelmed him. *Where are William and Celia?* He distracted himself from worrying by making methodical preparations. He covered the kitchen table with a layer of old newspaper and collected the scissors, some paper and a biro. He wondered whether to wear gloves—the Major was finicky about his hands, and ink had a habit of insinuating itself into every crevice—but in the event decided to sacrifice cleanliness to dexterity.

Since he had last seen it, most of the ribbon had fallen off the two spools and recombined in a tangle of knots and loops. He found what had been the right-hand spool and traced the unused ribbon back to the *yours faithfully.* He cut the ribbon at this point, which reduced the tangle by a quarter. That was progress.

Working back to what had been the left-hand spool was a laborious process. It was made harder by the standard of typing—deletions and/or repetitions were frequent. The first item—and therefore the last to be written—was the final draft of Celia's letter of resignation. It embarrassed him to read it. Next came a cluster of letters from Richard Prentisse, copies of which were no doubt on the files. He had written to his publisher and his agent. There was a particularly stinging letter to the local authority about the gross inefficiency of their dustmen. Major Dougal skimmed through the letters and felt increasingly despondent. What was the point of knowing what Richard had to say to his bank manager?

Then he struck pay dirt. He found a clamp of three identical letters, all dated August 10, thirteen days before Richard died. They differed only in their addresses—the advertising offices of the *Guardian, The Times,* and the *Daily Telegraph.* The letters confirmed telephone con-

156

versations and enclosed a check. The text of the advertisement, which was to run for three days in each newspaper, was as follows:

CORNER, *Alfred X: historian wishes to contact Harold Corner, born c. 1918 and son of the above. Please write c/o Box no. . . .*

Major Dougal noted down the text of the advertisement and the dates. He ran through the rest of the ribbon. There was nothing else of interest. Most of it was taken up with the article on von Kleist.

With a sigh of relief he pushed aside the ribbon, stood up and stretched. The ribbon could safely be destroyed, he decided: newspaper records were all the evidence they needed—always supposing they ever found a use for the evidence. He found a crumpled brown paper bag in the bin and wrapped the ribbon in it.

He scrubbed his hands at the kitchen sink, luxuriating in the foam from the washing-up liquid and the bite of the bristles of the nail brush. The discovery of the advertisement pleased him, but he had to admit it was almost certainly valueless. It lent support to the hypothesis that the enclosure that Richard had found in the *Encyclopedia Brittanica* linked Alfred Corner, Snowden's informant, with the murder case that had involved his son thirteen or fourteen years later. It also suggested that Harold Corner might have had something to do with Richard's death, if one first assumed that Corner had seen the advertisement.

A suggestion—not proof. Richard might have been following other lines of investigation. They were stymied by the old problem—they didn't know what the encyclopedia had concealed.

It puzzled him that they hadn't come across carbons of

the letters to the newspapers. Then he realized that Richard had probably kept them together with any other material he had on the subject. Whoever had killed him had scooped the jackpot.

In any case, it was all academic now. Looking for the ribbon was a harmless concession to one's curiosity; looking for Corner, on the other hand, could well be fatal.

He folded up the newspapers and stuffed them in the bin. It would be better not to mention this little adventure to William and Celia. It was unfortunate that he would have to admit to taking the ribbon, because Celia would sooner or later notice its absence. He would have to say that he had found nothing of interest on it, and destroyed it. It would make him look a hypocrite in Celia's eyes, but that couldn't be helped.

The telephone rang as he was washing his hands for the second time. He ran to answer it, leaving a trail of sudsy drops across the kitchen and down the hall.

To his disappointment it wasn't William but someone asking for him. The voice was a woman's, abrupt and deep toned.

"I'm sorry. Neither of them is here at present. Can I help? I'm William's father."

"You could ask him to ring up Ruth Guban when he gets in. He knows the number. If it's after midnight, tell him to ring tomorrow."

"Wait." The Major sensed she was about to put the phone down. "Is it about the Landis case? I . . . ah . . . know the background to that and could pass on a message."

"Don't worry," said Ruth Guban infuriatingly. "It's not urgent. In any case, I'd rather talk on someone else's phone bill. Good-bye."

158

A click came down the line from London, chased by the whine of the dialing tone. Major Dougal replaced the receiver and moodily returned to the kitchen sink.

Now what could Ruth Guban have to tell them? William had left his phone number with her on the off chance, but both he and Celia thought the writer had already given them all the information she had.

He wiped the water from the floor, washed his hands and poured himself a very small whisky. It was nearly half past ten. The evening had run out of options.

17

CELIA WAS IN a foul temper.

The taxi had dropped them outside St. John's Wood underground station. As they walked back to where they had parked the car, she announced that she planned to go to Reckless tonight and confront Corner. William suggested they talk about it first, and steered her into the Rossetti, a modern pub on the corner of the road where the car was parked. Her resolution held firm over two pints: she was tired of skulking—it was time to ask direct questions and get direct answers.

William's resistance appeared to crumble. But when they reached the car he grabbed her handbag, which contained both her money and her car keys, and took possession of the driver's seat. He said they weren't going anywhere but home to Plumford. If she tried to resist he would tie her up with his own shoelaces.

When she tried to get out from the passenger seat, he grabbed her wrist and wrenched her back. It was the first time she had ever seen the streak of physical violence in him directed toward herself. It terrified her: and that made her angry. She attacked him but he was stronger than she. In the end she spent the journey back to Plumford in the passenger seat. On top of everything, she had to suffer several hours of William's appalling driving.

160

She grew quieter during the final hour of the drive. William agreed to stop for coffee and a visit to the lavatory at a roadside café thirty miles south of Plumford. She didn't try to escape. The adrenalin had drained away from her now; and she was too tired to do anything about Corner tonight, even if she had been able to reach him. She could even admit, though not to William, that going to Reckless tonight might have been unwise. She derived a little consolation from spilling her first cup of coffee over William's trousers. Okay, it was petty. So was everything else since St. John's Wood. They were both behaving as if they were twenty years younger than they were.

She dropped off William at Uncle Ted's, refusing their invitation to come in. The Major looked haggard, she thought. Perhaps they should have phoned him from London. He was the worrying kind. She was surprised to hear that he had seen Margaret that evening. When Uncle Ted said that her stepmother was feeling her father's death more than any of them realized, surprise changed to anger: her father was hers to mourn, not Margaret's. The Major said good night, touched her cheek in a ghost of a caress and went back into the house.

William bent down to the window of the car. A cigarette tip glowed above his hand. "I'm sorry. I had to do it, you know? Will you come round tomorrow morning?"

"Perhaps," Celia said to both questions. She let out the clutch and pulled away. She could see William standing under the streetlamp near the Dougals' mirror gate in her rear mirror. His shoulders were slumped.

She slept badly, dreaming of flies with huge bellies and gaping jaws, and of people lying asleep under piles of bedclothes who turned out not to be people at all. She

161

felt better after a long bath, though her limbs and her mind both seemed one and a half times heavier than usual.

Margaret had prepared the sort of breakfast she used to make before Richard died. The kitchen table was properly laid. The meal had a certain formality about it. It was an edible olive branch.

They both ate far more scrambled eggs and bacon than they wanted. Margaret kept the conversation away from Jim and the teaching profession. She mentioned that she had decided to stay in Plumford for a while. Portuguese villas were all very well, but you couldn't trust the water or the police out there, could you? She added hesitantly that the death of someone you loved could make one a little impulsive for a while.

Celia agreed. She offered to finish clearing out her father's papers later on. That reminded Margaret: Mr. Chanter from the Champney Crucis bookshop was coming around at eleven to value the books. Would Celia care to show him round? Celia hastily pleaded another appointment, but softened the blow by asking if she could do any shopping for the weekend while she was out. She had no desire to resurrect the persona of Detective Constable Jones.

She drove into town and hurled herself among the Saturday morning shoppers who were already thronging the supermarket. Feeling rather less than real was something of an advantage under those conditions. She finished the shopping in half an hour. On impulse she went into the off-license and bought a bottle of Gordon's for Margaret and a bottle of Bell's for the Dougals. If you could have edible olive branches, there was no reason why you couldn't have drinkable ones too.

The tinny chimes of St. Clement's signaled half past

ten as she got back to the car. She drove up the hill to the Dougals'. Father and son were both in the front garden, staring at the Major's Ford Anglia and looking bemused.

Major Dougal came out on to the pavement as Celia drew up at the curb. He opened the door for her.

"I've never seen the car look so clean, Uncle Ted."

"Not just clean, my dear. De-rusted and resprayed. And that's just what's been done on the surface. Heaven only knows how William got them to do it so quickly. Usually they take months to repair a puncture."

William came over to join them. "It's almost a collector's car, you know. That's what the bloke from the garage said. Low mileage and very good condition for its age." He grinned at Major Dougal. "You should look upon it as an investment."

"And it works, too. Astonishing." The Major looked sternly at William. "We'll talk about the bill later."

Celia presented her bottle. "One for the larder. I had rather a lot the other night."

The Major led the way into the house. William lingered, running a finger along the gleaming blue paintwork. "I told my father what happened yesterday. Do you mind? He's in it too, you see. We can't insulate him from the risks."

Celia shook her head. "Maybe it's better. I'm sorry about last night's tantrum. You were right." She stopped on the threshold and looked back at him. "But if you ever lay a finger on me like that again, I promise you'll get worse than a cup of coffee."

They went into the sitting room. William left them to make some coffee. Major Dougal told her about his theft of the typewriter ribbon and the interesting, if inconclusive, evidence it had produced.

"Mind you," he finished, "I succumbed to temptation

163

yesterday. I suppose we all did, one way or another. But I haven't changed my mind. It would be absolute stupidity to take this any further." A flicker of embarrassment crossed his face as William came in with the coffee. "But there was one more development this morning, which you might as well know. Then we'll all be fair and square."

William passed round the cups and lit a cigarette. "Ruth Guban rang last night while we were out," he said. "She wouldn't talk to my father so I rang her this morning. Don't get excited—it's just a footnote really. It seems that she is writing a biography on Ralph Anderson, who was apparently the doyen of crime reporters between the wars. The family's given her access to his papers. He covered the Landis trial in 1932. Most of his notes add nothing to what we already know. Either the details came out in the press or they're tedious scraps like what the jurymen had for dinner. But he got hold of one story that was never written up. All Ruth could find was a few disconnected jottings. She dictated them to me over the phone. You'll see the name 'George'—she's pretty sure that he was the stringer in Cambridge for Anderson's paper."

Celia took the sheet of paper from him. No doubt Ruth Guban was being so obliging because she fancied William. She pushed the thought out of her mind: no point in being bitchy. She bent her head over the paper to prevent him from seeing her face.

Trial in second day. With George to pub in King St. Had been contacted by a man who called himself Tom. Claimed to have served with L. in the war. Nervy chap: lungs bad. Shell-shocked? Face the color of lard. Had telephoned George yesterday at the office. L. a sergeant 1917-18; Tom

in same platoon. L. a f—b—and deeply involved in all the
rackets. Commissioned because he agreed to give false evi-
dence at court-martial of officer from another regiment.
Tom admits just gossip—no hard evidence—but "I know
Landis. That's the sort of man he is." L. said to have
boasted that he had seen photograph of defendant's
widow—beautiful and wealthy—and that he planned to
look her up after the war.

Good story but can't use it. Tom refused to let himself be
quoted. Would in any case make bad witness, even if he
lives much longer. And couldn't publish until after trial.
George . . .

As Celia looked up, William said: "It was written in
Anderson's homemade shorthand. One sheet torn from a
notebook. If there was any more, it hasn't survived."

"It gives us a connection," Celia said slowly. "Between
the court-martial and Muriel Hinton's murder. It's far
better than that kid happening to be the posthumous son
of Alfred. It hangs together. Landis helped to get Corner
executed. He filed away the wealthy widow for postwar
reference. By the time he traced the Hinton family, Alexandra Corner was probably dead herself. Muriel wasn't
the marrying kind. I expect he put Bea on the back
burner—she was pretty and in a way her youth was an
advantage. I wouldn't mind betting he got her that job in
the motor showroom. All part of digging himself in as a
friend of the family. Then after they were married he
turned his attention to Muriel's bank balance—and got
carried away."

"It's feasible." Major Dougal absently touched his hair,
which Celia knew was often a sign of doubt in him. "But
it's very tenuous. It stands out a mile that Anderson
thought Tom could be either malicious or mad or both."

165

"Why did he let the story go?" Celia demanded. "Surely he could have found someone to corroborate it?"

"It would have been difficult." William put down his coffee cup. "John and Beatice wouldn't want to talk about it; and Mrs. Hinton had clammed up. Tom was a thoroughly unreliable witness in the first place. And of course the whole matter was *sub judice*. Anderson must have known how the judge would have reacted if there was even a hint that the defendant had conspired to kill the man who could have been his brother-in-law. He wouldn't risk a prosecution for contempt of court."

"I can think of one other reason why Anderson took it no further." Major Dougal coughed modestly, as if disclaiming any originality in the idea. "The only way the dirt could be made to stick would be with War Office cooperation. He'd need access to the files of Corner and Landis—and to the records of the Judge Advocate General's department."

William nodded. "The War Office was hypersensitive about courts-martial at that time. There was a lot of public agitation about them in the 1920s. The Army Council fought them all the way, but Ramsay MacDonald's government pushed through a bill in 1930 that made treachery and mutiny the only offenses punishable by death in the army. Corner was shot for desertion. Even if the case was entirely above board, the army wouldn't have opened up its files for the press. But this one would have been dynamite: an intentional miscarriage of justice for political purposes, though Anderson can't have known that."

"As I said, my dear," the Major said gently to Celia, "all this is just a footnote. Though I suppose it's just possible that whatever your father found in the encyclopedia connected Landis with Corner's court-martial."

166

Celia forced a smile. "I keep thinking: Daddy would have loved all this." She shivered. "Fifty years ago makes it all seem safe. I almost forgot that four people have died in the last couple of months. It's as if evil's like radioactivity."

"Nuclear waste." William's face was grave. "Still lethal after thousands of years. Now what?"

There was an instant's silence as the conversation shifted into another gear. The three of them were all at ease now the discussion had reached the present. They jarred on one another. Celia was conscious that, just behind her eyes, a hairy little man was lying on his side half concealed by a flowery duvet, while flies patroled the airspace above them. Yesterday she had seen her first dead person. *Once seen, never forgotten* thrummed through her mind like the rhythm of rails beneath a train. She listened and spoke, smiled and frowned, just as if nothing had happened. But the rhythm was there in the background, remorselessly carrying her into the darkness.

She watched William closely, anxious to trace even a hint that his mind was running along the same lines. He was sitting placidly, cross-legged on the sofa, with a cigarette dangling from the corner of his mouth, like Bogart playing Buddha. He saw her looking and smiled at her with his eyes. For an instant Celia was visited by the odd fancy that there was nothing whatever behind those eyes: no thoughts, no rhythms of memory, and no feelings. She shook her head to clear it.

Major Dougal assumed that the movement meant she was dissatisfied with the shape of their discussion. "You're right," he said sternly. "We're just muddling along. If neither of you minds, I think we should go through the whole business and sort out what we know and what we can suppose."

He took their silence for consent. "All right. Fact: Landis killed his sister-in-law; his motive was primarily greed; but there may also have been a desire for self-protection if she'd stumbled across his putative involvement in the judicial murder of her other brother-in-law. Supposition: it must have been traumatic for Harry, already an orphan, to lose both his nearest remaining relatives and his home—and to be at the center of a murder case. Fact number two: Harry went on to become a big wheel in the bureaucratic machine, which ultimately administers our security services. I think we can take whatsisname's—Toad's?—word for that. Supposition number two: Harry eventually discovered the facts about father's death and has done his best to conceal them ever since. I think he did that for a number of reasons, both personal and professional. Filial piety, for one—the fact he's kept his father's surname and even mentions him proudly in his *Who's Who* entry is significant. If you're an orphaned boy, who better to set up on a pedestal than a dead hero-father? For another, the truth about Alfred wouldn't have helped Harry's career. His sort of civil servant tends to vote Conservative."

Celia interrupted hesitantly. "It might be even more important for him to keep it from his wife and children. After his sort of upbringing, he's probably invested a lot of emotional capital in them. He'd want to protect them. But why didn't he simply destroy the file?"

"Because it's very difficult to destroy any record of that sort without someone noticing." The Major smiled. "Chap where I used to work had a pet saying about it: 'Burning alive is safer than cremation.' "

William stubbed out his cigarette. "We don't know it was *Harry* who buried that file. Hundreds of people must

168

have had a vested interest in keeping its contents quiet, over the years. It may have happened seventy-odd years ago, but it's still a dirty little story."

"That's perfectly true as far as it goes. But if our later suppositions are to make sense, Corner must have had something to do with the cover-up. Fact number three: Beatrice Landis, or Hinton, was to give her side of the Landis case for a TV documentary after fifty years of silence. Supposition number three: her accidental death, before she could do this, was in fact murder, planned— and possibly executed—by Harry Corner. Now the average dra—, civil servant I mean, has no interest whatsoever in the Landis case. Therefore, if it was murder, Harry is our most likely candidate as prime mover."

"Why?" Celia's voice was curt. Uncle Ted was enjoying the piecing together of his four-dimensional jigsaw puzzle. He seemed to have forgotten that people were involved.

The Major waved a hand. "Harry's a respectable married man. Quite possibly he's hoping for a knighthood. The family murder would be almost as embarrassing as his father's court-martial. Remember, Beatice must have known something about the court-martial. Corner couldn't run the risk of her bringing that up as well before an audience of millions. Chaps like him live in a hothouse world. Reputation is absolutely everything. They're all Caesar's wives. But—if Beatrice was murdered—there might have been another motive. I know she was cleared at the trial, but suppose Harry had his own reasons for thinking she wasn't innocent. The victim—his Aunt Muriel—must have been like a surrogate mother to him. Hating someone who's done you an injury can be a very long-lived emotion. Anyway, that's all pure

169

speculation. Fact number four: Richard buys Alfred's old encyclopedia; he probably didn't know that Beatrice was its last owner, but something he found inside *med to mum* convinced him there was a connection between Snowden's spy and the Landis case. Facts numbers five and six: he starts researching the Landis case and he advertises for Harry Corner. Fact number seven:—"

"My father dies," said Celia in a small, hard voice.

The Major's enthusiasm died. "Quite so," he said. As Celia watched, the furrows on his face seemed to grow deeper. He glanced at Aunt Anne's photograph. "I'm sorry, my dear. One gets carried away. Absolutely unpardonable in the circumstances."

Celia pressed her back hard against the chair, to remind her she was here and now in the real world. "Please go on, Uncle Ted. It's time I got used to it."

It took a moment or two before he was sufficiently reassured to do so. He continued in a lower, less confident tone. Their fourth supposition was that Richard had been murdered, bolstered by their knowledge of his character and the absence of any of the material he had gathered on Landis or Corner.

William said suddenly: "I don't know how Corner did it, but he has a taste for bizarre detail. He must have taken one big risk—writing to one of the box numbers."

"He didn't necessarily have to write to the box number. Every big newspaper employs people who work for two masters. Box numbers aren't *that* secret. And remember, Richard's letter to M.o.D. about Corner three years ago would have been logged. Young Harry would have had plenty of time to acquire information on Richard." He looked directly at Celia: "You know that interview he gave on Radio Four last April? He talked a lot about his working methods—including the fact that he was very

170

secretive during the early stages of a book, and put as little on paper as possible. I'm sure Harry noticed that."

"I wish I knew *how* he did it," Celia said jerkily. "It shouldn't be important, but for some reason it is."

"I can understand that." The Major's eyes flicked involuntarily sideways toward the photograph on the mantelpiece. "Fact number eight," he said doggedly: "I contact an old colleague who tries to get hold of Alfred's file; and number nine: the colleague, er, goes west. Supposition—Oh God, I can't remember the number—the first event caused the second."

William smoothly interrupted before the Major stopped of his own accord. (Celia wondered how that sort of sensitivity could coexist with his coldness about Nick's death.) "And the same pattern holds true for Nick, of course. But I do wonder how they got hold of him—unless Jack Toad was responsible."

"Nick didn't know anything about Corner," Major Dougal pointed out. "None of us did at that point. A man in Corner's position always has his minders. Nick made no special effort to conceal what he was doing."

"We don't know what happened to your colleague." William looked shrewdly at his father. "But has it struck you that the other three murders have very little in common between them? A restrained little accident . . . a suicide with lots of quirky, almost fussy touches . . . and a textbook contract murder." He stopped abruptly and reached for his cigarettes. "But that's all academic. The problem is what we do now."

With uncomfortable clarity the words took shape among Celia's thoughts: *His mind took him somewhere he didn't want to go. Or to something he didn't want to say. To me? To Uncle Ted?*

"As I see it," William continued, "we have only two

options." A qualification hung unspoken in the air: two *legal* options. "We can do nothing, and leave Corner to the judgment of . . . ah . . . providence. Or we can attack him frontally through the law or the press."

"That would be doomed to failure," Major Dougal said flatly. "We've got a few facts and suppositions, but nothing that constitutes proof. Just grounds for libel. And remember his position: he would be able to muzzle an accusation like ours with the minimum of publicity. All we would achieve—"

Celia finished it for him: "would be our own destruction by letting him know we were on to him." Her mouth twisted in disgust. "We've been here before, Uncle Ted. On Tuesday night."

The Major looked steadily at her. "There's one difference: someone else has died."

"You don't have to rub it in." Celia glanced at her watch. "Look, I must go. I promised Margaret I'd be in for lunch. You're right, of course. We've only had the one option all along, haven't we? Let's leave Corner to providence."

She left shortly afterward. William came out with her to the car. There was no point in saying what she planned to do. It was her quarrel—hers to settle without involving anyone but herself and the other principal. She had to know the truth—and the only person who could give it to her was Corner. Once she had the truth, she would make her own justice. Protecting herself was not important. She felt no anger—only that calmness that comes after making a major decision. Trying to recruit the Dougals would not only be unfair to them but counterproductive for her.

But she was glad William was seeing her off. There was

more chance he would talk while they were by themselves. "What were you going to say about the murders?" she demanded. "After you said there was very little in common between them."

William shrugged. "Just speculation. If Beatrice was killed, it was done very economically and with very little risk for the murderer. But your father's death must have been a chancy business to organize—and it's almost as if Corner enjoyed all the little flourishes, like the marked copy of Schopenhauer. Nick's death made no pretense to be anything but murder. Corner might have hired someone to do it, or he might have done it himself."

"Well?" Celia prompted. "We know all that."

"It struck me that Corner is no longer killing merely to accomplish one particular purpose. He's taking risks; he's trying out variations." William paused, groping for words. "I think he's gone a bit berserk. He's having fun. Murder's become a habit for him."

18

CORNER WAS INSANE.

Major Dougal considered the proposition and found it good. He turned left on to the Plumford bypass and accelerated up through the gears. The Anglia responded gallantly: it topped seventy with hardly a rattle.

Corner was insane. That's what had been in the back of William's mind when he mentioned how different the murders were. Not insane in the standard medical sense, whatever that might be—just trigger-happy. After his desk-bound career, the fact that killing could solve problems must have operated on him with the force of a religious revelation.

It was only a matter of time before Corner found the common link between Richard Prentisse, Colonel Blaines, and Nick Marston. And then he would turn his attention—and his newfound expertise—to the Dougals and Celia.

There was one alternative. The other appealed to him even less. Before very long his goddaughter was going to hunt out Corner for herself, probably armed to the teeth with a carving knife. She hadn't changed—as a child she had been determined to fight her own battles, motivated by a wholly unworkable concept of justice.

Major Dougal had considered the problem and had

174

come up with the only possible solution—or, to be more precise, the option that had the fewest evils in attendance. He was older than Celia; he had both the experience and the means of killing; he knew something of the psychology of dragons.

Moreover, if matters went awry, Corner might look no further than Major Dougal for the common link. Celia and William need never be involved.

He glossed over the flaw in this argument: Celia and William would be even more likely to get themselves involved if he was killed. But he didn't intend to get himself killed.

He pulled into the slow lane to allow the black Rover behind him to overtake. For an instant he had been tempted to stay put, just to aggravate the Rover's driver. But that would not only have been childish, it would have infringed one of the basic rules—*don't draw attention to yourself unnecessarily.*

Acting now had another advantage. Corner would almost certainly be in the country for the weekend; he would be relaxed, particularly after Nick Marston's death, and unlikely to be on his guard. The Major reckoned he had a better than average chance of taking Corner by surprise. The longer he left it, the slimmer the chance would become.

He looked at his watch: it was two-thirty. Barring hold-ups he should be near Reckless in a couple of hours. He had no fears he would be missed at home. Celia was clearing out her father's study, and William had decided to spend the afternoon walking. The Major had mentioned at lunch that he might take the car out for a spin this afternoon. It was unlikely that anyone would worry about him, at least until the early evening.

He nudged the speedometer up to seventy-five. He had

175

always found it a sound operational rule to allow as little time as possible between the decision to act and the act itself.

At least he wouldn't have to worry about minders. He chuckled at the memory of that altruistic piece of disinformation. William and Celia had swallowed it effortlessly. Who did they think Corner was working for? An organization with the manpower of the KGB? It was perfectly obvious how Corner had got on to young Marston—the Major had known ever since he had heard the Consort House address. The porters there were paid a comfortable tax-free bonus to keep a fatherly eye on certain of the flats. It was highly unlikely that Corner would have any sort of bodyguard down at Reckless. Civil servants liked their privacy as much as anyone else.

Corner's family was another matter. He had to consider the probability that Corner's wife and at least one of his daughters would be there. It needn't necessarily be a drawback. Quite the reverse.

A lifetime's industry was neatly lined up in twelve black plastic sacks, drawn up in two ranks of six, and four cardboard boxes. They would have to wheedle the dustmen to take away the extra sacks. Celia intended to keep the boxes for herself. She stared at her filthy hands, ruefully aware that whatever she did she would regret it. If she kept all her father's papers they would encumber her for the rest of her life. On the other hand, something among those she threw away would later prove to have been indispensable.

She smiled at Margaret as her stepmother edged round the flank of the plastic sacks. "That's it, I think. I'll pile them up by the dustbins. Do you think dustmen take bribes?"

176

"Bound to, dear," said Margaret absently. "Mrs. Gann saw Jeff—he's the one who drives their truck—in a great big Mercedes the other weekend. Do you happen to know where Ted is? I've been trying to ring him all afternoon."

Celia shook her head. "He didn't mention this morning that he was going out. William said something about having a walk this afternoon, so that's why he isn't at home. I said I'd have a drink with him this evening. I could ask Uncle Ted to ring you if I see him."

"It doesn't matter. Nothing important." Margaret glanced helplessly round the study. "I don't know what I shall *do* with this room when all the books and things have gone. Would you like some tea?"

Celia followed her stepmother downstairs. Now why did Margaret want to ring Uncle Ted? And why was she being so girlishly vague about it?

She called for William at six o'clock. It always gave her pleasure that she was the one who called to take him out. It was a healthy reversal of the traditional roles.

The front door was on the latch, and she walked straight in. William emerged from his bedroom at the end of the corridor, vigorously toweling his hair.

"Sorry, I forgot the time," he said. "I must have walked seven miles *and* I fell in a ditch."

He retreated into his room, leaving the door open, which Celia interpreted as an invitation to follow. As she stood on the threshold two realizations jolted her: she hadn't been in here for ten years; and the room appeared to have changed in only one way during the intervening decade—it had grown smaller.

There was the same Moroccan bedspread on the narrow single bed and a jumble of faded posters on the walls, which illustrated with unflattering accuracy the pictorial enthusiasms of William's teens and early twenties. Two walls were lined with four-foot-high shelves. Celia glanced at the ones nearest the door. She saw a well-thumbed copy of a William book, a novel by Hermann Hesse, two books on the First World War, and the complete Sherlock Holmes short stories.

William buttoned up his shirt, tucked it modestly into his trousers and combed his hair. His eyes found hers in the mirror. "I know. It's a perfect time capsule. There's everything from team photographs to Enid Blyton, on top of the wardrobe. I really must clear it out. Funny to think of my father keeping it like this for all those years."

It was funny, Celia agreed; and it was also strange to be in William's bedroom—it conferred a spurious intimacy on their relationship. "That reminds me," she said in an attempt to bring the conversation into safer waters. "Margaret said she tried to ring Uncle Ted this afternoon. I could leave a note asking him to call her when he gets in."

The comb stopped, its teeth deep in William's damp hair. "When did Margaret ring?"

"Apparently she rang several times, starting just after lunch. I got her to tell me why in the end. Your father's asked her out to dinner, and she wants to pin him down to a date as soon as possible. Quaint, isn't it?"

She had expected to see her smile reflected on William's face. It wasn't every day one discovered that two such antagonists as Margaret and Uncle Ted were secretly planning a romantic candle-lit evening together. But William's face was serious. He tossed the comb onto the chest of drawers and turned to look at her.

"My father said he might try the car sometime this afternoon. He implied he was only going to drive a few

178

miles. But if Margaret's been trying to get hold of him all afternoon, he could have been gone for four hours."

"He might have had a breakdown." Celia knew she was being deliberately obtuse, chiefly for the sake of her own peace of mind. "There could be dozens of reasons—"

The harsh ring of the telephone interrupted her. William slipped past her into the hall and picked up the receiver. His side of the short conversation revealed little, for it largely consisted of "But," "I see," and "Where did you say?"

William slammed the receiver back on its rest. "He said he'd run into an old army friend in Newmarket, and they were going to have dinner in Bury St. Edmunds." He mimicked his father's voice: " 'You must remember old Tubby Riley?' He said he was in a hurry and wouldn't let me ask anything. Not a call box—at least, there were no pips."

"It could be true," Celia said, hoping it was. "I think having the car back has given him a new lease on life."

William ignored her. He went into the kitchen and rummaged in the drawer under the draining board until he found a torch. He took it into the bathroom. Celia trailed after him. She was beginning to get angry at his neglect.

William opened the airing cupboard and took out a wooden pole with an iron hook at one end. He gave Celia the torch to hold and, as he did so, caught sight of her face. "Sorry," he said. "It's just an idea. I think my father's lying, and it might help us to find out."

He used the pole to open the trapdoor into the roof space and to pull down the sliding aluminum ladder. He climbed up into the loft, dislodging a shower of dust, which drifted down onto the bathroom carpet.

179

Celia followed him up the ladder until she was half in the loft. Most of it was unboarded. There was a water tank visible to the left. William's torch moved erratically over a pile of dusty trunks stacked in the alcove to the right of the chimney breast. He tugged them gently away from the wall, along the line of the rafters. The fitful illumination reduced him to a shadow for most of the time. His voice came back to Celia, punctuated with deep intakes of breath and the scrape of metal on wood.

"I used to come up here quite a lot when I was a kid . . . rummaging around . . . had my first Gold Flake sitting on this trunk when I was twelve . . . I was sick in a top hat . . . I wonder if my father's missed it yet . . . one of the bricks here was loose . . . one day I got it out . . . there's a little niche . . . I poked my hand through and it came back sooty . . . must have connected with the sitting-room chimney . . . ventilation of some sort, maybe when we had an open fire . . . I thought I'd use it as a hiding place . . . but when I came back a few weeks later, someone else had already put the idea into effect . . . my father."

The last few words were muffled. William had pulled the trunks far enough from the wall for him to be able to insert himself between them and the chimney breast. He bent down, and the light of the torch abruptly vanished.

"What was there?" Celia called after him.

William backed out of the space and, leaving the trunks where they were, walked warily over the rafters to the trapdoor. Apart from the torch he was empty handed. His hands were black; his shirt and his still-damp hair were coated with brickdust.

"There was a black metal cashbox," he said quietly, with a slight emphasis on the verb. "It was locked, but one day I found my father's keys on the bureau. Nosy lit-

180

tle bugger, wasn't I? It contained a Browning GP35, and twenty-six rounds to go with it."

The sun edged its way through the clouds that had been obscuring it and coated the road with yellow splendor. At precisely the same moment, Major Dougal reached the speed restriction sign on the outskirts of the city. He obediently slackened speed. St. Albans, he felt, was putting on its best clothes to welcome its latest visitor.

He follow the A414 into the town center. The pavements were thronged with Saturday afternoon shoppers who spilled on to the road in their haste to spend their money before the shops closed. The Ford Anglia trundled sedately through the obstacles and turned down Holywell Hill. The road crossed the river Ver. The Major, momentarily distracted by the improbably rustic wooden tower of St. Stephen's church, nearly aborted both his car and his mission by colliding with the battered Transit van in front of him.

Shortly afterward, the white facade of the Breakspeare Arms appeared on the left-hand side. Major Dougal's concentration wavered: it looked exactly the same as it had twenty-five years ago. A forty-eight-hour span of memory presented itself in a single, disturbing burst. They had dumped William on the Prentisses and enjoyed a blessedly childless weekend at the hotel. Except it hadn't been entirely blessed: a demanding young ghost, lurking in the corners of their minds just beyond the range of reason, had haunted them both for the whole weekend. Now he had another ghost here. *Anne.*

He drove on for another hundred yards, took a left and a right and parked the car in a public car park. He took his suitcase from the boot and walked back to the hotel. A sentimental impulse drove him to ignore the front entrance; he made his way round to the courtyard at the back of the building. Anne had liked that courtyard. As he came through the archway the past was annihilated, like darkness at the flick of a lightswitch. The cobblestones had been overlaid with asphalt. The decaying stables on the right had disappeared. The car park had swollen like a gray tide across their foundations and rolled on over what had once been the garden. In the corner by the old coach house was a cluster of cast-iron tables, painted white and topped with brightly colored beach umbrellas. A zigzagging fire escape and chains of colored bulbs had turned the back of the hotel into a vertical snakes-and-ladders board. He realized with relief that it was no more its previous self than he was.

The Major turned his back on the courtyard and went into the hotel. The reception desk was at the far end of the hall, near the front door. There was no one there. The establishment was wrapped in the postprandial stupor that enveloped all but the liveliest hotels in the late afternoon. He rapped the bell sharply. The sound swam sluggishly up the purple carpet of the stairs.

While he waited, Major Dougal glanced at the leaflets displayed on the top of the desk. The Breakspeare was no longer a glorified pub that offered accommodation almost as an afterthought. It was now a fully fledged hotel, a member of a nationwide chain, whose restaurant served countless variants on the theme of steak and chips, each of which was garnished with a Continental name.

The stairs creaked behind him. A fat young man was slowly descending, clinging to the banisters as if he was afraid that he would otherwise bounce uncontrollably from tread to tread. He was dark haired and swarthy skinned. His clothes—a black three-piece suit worn over

182

a white shirt whose collar was held tight against his neck by a thin black tie—added a touch of sinister formality to his appearance.

"Good afternoon," Major Dougal said. "My name is Harrell. I telephoned just after lunch to book a room for tonight."

"Yes," the fat young man agreed lugubriously. "You did."

"Perhaps," the Major suggested with a touch of asperity, "you would like to show me where it is."

But the fat young man was not to be hurried. First he made the Major sign the register. He queried the false address, not because it was false but because he found it difficult to read. Major Dougal paid in advance for the room, explaining that he might have to leave early in the morning. He could have used one of Harrell's credit cards, but decided that cash would be safer.

The rotund black body of the hotel employee wheezed up the stairs. The Major, carrying his own suitcase—that was another thing that had changed—followed behind, unsuccessfully fighting the temptation to draw smug comparisons between his own physical condition and that of this man who was half his age.

The room looked out over the rear of the hotel. The pattern of the wallpaper—a red bird pecking a blue bird against a nightmare background of jungle greens—was repeated not only on the curtains but on the bedspread as well. The room was equipped with a color television, its own bathroom, an electric kettle with one cup, two sachets of instant coffee, and a single tea bag, and a radio that was apparently, though mysteriously, capable of acting as a babysitter, should Major Dougal require this facility. More importantly, the fire escape was within easy reach of the broad sash window.

Major Dougal did not unpack. The telephone number of a local car-hire firm had been prominently displayed on the notice board beside the reception desk. He dialed the number from his room and arranged to pick up a Morris Marina at six. He was irritated to discover that the garage, whatever time you received a car from them, would charge you as if you had picked it up at 8 A.M.. Still, Harrell's Barclaycard would have to bear the burden. The argument in favor of getting another car was a strong one: if by any chance he left a trail after this evening, it would be as well to make it as muddy as possible.

Next he went on a shopping trip. It was difficult to know what he would need—the evening ahead was such an unknown quantity that the only certainty was that he would have to improvise. He bought a torch, paying as much attention to its weight and the way it sat in his hand as he did to its beam; it might have to act as a truncheon. He bought three maps of the area, including the 1:2500 OS map, which actually showed the Old Rectory by name. A thermos flask seemed a sensible investment—he could fill it in his room. In a camping shop he found a lined waterproof jacket with deep, strong pockets, and five yards of thin nylon rope.

When he had finished it was nearly time to pick up the car. He filled in the gap by making a leisurely circuit of the ungainly cathedral. He reached Holywell Hill by way of Sumpter Yard and walked down past the hotel to the garage. He picked up the bright blue Morris Marina and parked it in a side road near the hotel. When he got back to the Breakspeare it was a quarter past six.

He rang William from his bedroom, keeping the conversation as short as possible. The story of a chance meeting with Tubby Riley was the best he could do; at

184

least it had the advantage of being uncheckable—Tubby Riley had met a sniper's bullet in Aden in 1966.

His motives for making the call were mixed. He reasoned that it would stop William and Celia worrying about him. They might not entirely believe the Tubby Riley story, but there was absolutely no way they could know what he was really doing. Besides it gave him a chance to hear William's voice. He must be growing paternally soft in his old age.

At half past six it was time to go. He took the Browning from his suitcase, loaded thirteen rounds in the magazine and zipped the remaining thirteen in the inside pocket of his waterproof jacket. The automatic itself fitted comfortably in one of the buttoned outside pockets. The extra weight of two or three pounds dragged the jacket down against his right shoulder. He checked in the mirror: the jacket was bulky enough to conceal the distortion.

He distributed his purchases in the other pockets and in a carrier bag. He sorted through the remaining contents of the suitcase: there was nothing here that could betray him, if he was forced to abandon it.

The sash window was the last detail. He disengaged the catch and raised it. It moved easily, but had an unnerving tendency to screech at the beginning of its run. He fetched the soap from the bathroom and greased as much of the frame as he could reach. When he tried again the screech was reduced to a sigh. Good enough, he decided. With luck there wouldn't be any need to use this relatively undignified way of getting back into the hotel.

Major Dougal methodically rechecked all his dispositions. He saved the pistol until last. He was standing there, with the Browning in one hand and its box magazine in the other, when there was a gentle tap on the door.

19

"YOU'RE OVERREACTING," Celia said firmly. "Just because Uncle Ted had a gun ten years ago or more, it doesn't mean he has one now."

The harsh strip light in the kitchen gave William's pallor a bluish tinge. "I'm not talking about ten years ago," he snapped. "The box was up there on Thursday afternoon."

"You checked?"

William looked slightly awkward. "Just in case. I thought it might be useful to know if it was still in the house. The box was locked, of course, but the weight was right."

Celia sat down suddenly at the table. "So Uncle Ted's driven off somewhere with his gun. And you think he's gone to find Corner. But after all he said about letting sleeping dogs lie, *why?*"

A match flared; William sucked the flame into a cigarette. He stared accusingly at her through the smoke. "Because he knew that you—" he stabbed the glowing tip in her direction "—would go looking for Corner if he didn't. He's protecting you." There was a pause before William added: "And me, of course."

Celia picked up her car keys. "What are we waiting for?"

"Wait." William ran his hand through his hair, leaving a trail of damp spikes protruding from his scalp. "My father's almost certainly gone to Reckless, right? He's armed. I think we can assume he's not going to reason with Corner."

The next piece in the pattern followed logically; there was no need for William to spell it out. But belief, as so often, lagged behind logic. Celia struggled to leave it there.

"He could have taken it in self-defense. As a sort of insurance policy. Uncle Ted wouldn't *do* that sort of thing."

"We've no idea what he'd do. Or what he's done. I never realized how little I knew about him." William stubbed out his half-smoked cigarette in the ashtray, with a force that suggested that he was grinding it in the face of his own ignorance. "But we do know that he's not a fool. And there's every reason to suspect that he's perfectly aware of what he's doing."

Celia wondered why she could contemplate with equanimity the idea of herself killing Corner, while the thought of Uncle Ted doing it, largely for her sake, filled her with revulsion. Her mouth was dry. She went to the sink and rinsed it with water. She turned back to William.

"What are you saying?"

"That if we rushed over there we'd only complicate things for him." He tried to laugh; it came out like a rusty hiccup. "I remember Tubby Riley. He got killed in Aden when I was about fourteen."

It was Celia's turn to try to laugh. "Ironic, isn't it? He's the fledgling who's left the nest and we're the two anxious parents, waiting and worrying."

187

"If he doesn't come back," William said softly, "at least we'll know why."

The discussion sputtered between them for another twenty minutes. It was like the urge to scratch a mosquito bite, in the full knowledge that doing so would only make it worse. They always returned to the same point: any intervention on their part would be far more likely to harm Major Dougal than to help him.

"Come on," said Celia briskly when they reached the problem for the sixth time. "This is stupid. We'll just have to wait here until something happens. Why don't we cook a meal?"

Celia bullied William into laying bare the resources of the larder. They made a complex and indigestible meal involving three sorts of salads, a pound of sausages, a tin of baked beans, jacket potatoes, a hunk of Stilton, and half a pound of mushrooms. Neither of them ate more than half a dozen mouthfuls; but the enterprise occupied their hands and at least part of their minds. Celia drew strength from one source only: William's misery was even worse than hers. She was obliged to devote a lot of her energy to hustling him along; it diminished the amount she was able to spend on worrying.

When neither of them could maintain the pretense of eating any longer, they washed up with meticulous care. Celia made a pot of coffee and led the way into the sitting room. Each of them took a corner of the sofa, with the tray stationed on the neutral territory between them.

The silence reminded Celia of a dentist's waiting room. William smoked continuously, as if his life depended upon it. Celia wanted to put her arms around him, but the last ten years and the coffee tray held them apart as effectively as barbed wire and a minefield. She was haunted by the idea that this was her fault. If she had

188

been content to accept her father's death, none of this would have happened.

She draped her left arm on her lap so that she could see her watch without appearing to do so. The white face, the black Roman numerals, and the spidery hands acquired a sinister life of their own, animated by the ticking heartbeat behind them.

At last they began to talk. Only one subject appeared to hold any interest for William—what they would do if Major Dougal failed to return. He worried it like a loose tooth. Each plan was less feasible and more violent than its predecessor.

The fifth plan involved the formation of what seemed to be a small squad of amateur commandos. William discussed the weaponry they might require with a fierce, obsessive concentration. Celia remembered that firearms had been one of the few interests shared by Uncle Ted and William during the latter's teens.

Just as he was debating the respective merits of Kalashnikov and FN rifles, there were two brisk rings on the front doorbell.

Major Dougal rammed the magazine into the butt of the pistol and slid the automatic into his pocket. As he did so, he moved toward the door. He slid against the wall, positioning himself so he would be behind the door if it burst open. His hand closed round the Browning.

"Who is it?" he asked quietly.

"The manager." A wheezing sigh lent credibility to the words.

The Major glanced behind him, checking that the room was in a fit state for a stranger to see it. He unlatched the Yale lock and swung open the door.

The fat young man stood in the corridor, rocking

189

gently to and fro like a balloon in a draught. He held out the open hotel register and a biro with one hand and petulantly tapped the page with the other. His brown eyes stared accusingly at the Major.

"You forgot to make a note of the registration number of your car."

Major Dougal sighed, "I came by public transport."

The hire car handled better than the Major had expected. Downhill on a motorway, he reckoned he would be able to push it up to 100 m.p.h. The 1300 engine wouldn't like it, but it could cope, for a while at least.

It was unlikely he would need the facility, but his mind nevertheless recorded it. The evening ahead was necessarily going to contain a great deal of improvisation and almost any fact, in a context of uncertainty, might sooner or later prove to be useful. One fact about the Morris Marina had made him chose it over the other models available: it had a remarkably capacious boot.

His route took him south and west of St. Albans, and away from main roads. Though the map had prepared him for what lay ahead, he was surprised by the emptiness of the Hertforshire countryside. It was difficult to believe that the northern suburbs of London were a few miles beyond the southern horizon. He followed narrow, unmarked lanes, which twisted round hillocks and plunged in and out of little valleys. He passed farmhouses whose windows were already beginning to glow as the twilight crept across the fields around them. There were few cars on the road.

Navigation was the only problem. The existing roads were difficult to correlate with those on the maps. Major Dougal had a good sense of direction, but found it hard to cope after a few miles in this maze of lanes. The signposts were malicious rather than helpful. One directed him left, with the information that Reckless was eight miles away; the next signpost sent him to the right, and Reckless had somehow retreated eleven miles away; at the third intersection, the signpost mentioned eight names, but Reckless was not among them; at the fourth intersection there was no signpost at all.

Major Dougal drove on for another two miles until he found a village whose name was also recorded on the map. He discovered he was three and a half miles from Reckless. From then on he ignored the signposts. Ten minutes later he reached the village.

In theory, he knew Reckless from having studied the map. The village was the shape of a straggling capital T, surrounded by a few blotches, which signified outlying farms. The main road—or rather the larger of the two lanes—formed the crosspiece of the T. Where it joined the upright, there was a lozenge-shaped village green. The church and the Old Rectory were about a hundred and fifty yards away from the junction, facing onto the smaller of the lanes.

As always the reality was subtly different from the schematic version on the map. Major Dougal was expecting a pub at one end of the village green but not the girdle of cars that were parked bumper to bumper around the lozenge. On two sides of the green were terraced cottages, originally intended for agricultural laborers by a nineteenth-century landlord. Now the cottages were crisply whitewashed; many of them had double glazing on the windows and sported front doors that their owners no doubt believed were Georgian.

Metroland, the Major realized, had leapfrogged over the intervening countryside into Reckless. He could see the lights of housing estates, unmarked on the map, twin-

191

kling on the rising ground behind the church and also beyond the pub. A train rattled by in the distance: Reckless
must be one of the stations on what used to be called the
Bedpan Line.

He turned right into the upright of the T and drove
slowly to the church. The Old Rectory was just beyond it,
set back in its own drive. The Major parked on the road,
automatically ensuring that the tall box hedge on the
right of the wrought-iron gates made the car invisible
from the house. It was one of those tiny but irritating decisions that had once been second nature to Major Dougal, but no less irritating for that. They were irritating
because they were imponderable: there was no way of
knowing whether in the long run it might be safer to park
out of sight of the house or of the road. They were also
irritating because a miscalculation, one time in a thou-
sand, could prove fatal.

The gravel crunched beneath his feet as he walked up
the short drive. Now the time had come, the inessentials
had miraculously been evacuated from his mind. He was
concious of many things, but all of them were relevant to
his reason for being here.

The weight of the Browning slapped against his thigh.
The garden had been mostly laid to lawns—probably the
housing estate had eaten a slice of it. There was very little
cover. Apart from the main gates, there were two other
exits: a tradesmen's entrance, which the Major had noticed as he passed it in the car, and an iron gate that led
directly into the churchyard.

The house itself was a plain, early Victorian building
with large blank windows and an almost puritanical absence of gracefulness. The brick walls were unrendered,
which accentuated the building's severity. Five or six
bedrooms, Major Dougal estimated, and perhaps two or

three bathrooms. It was an impressive—and doubtless valuable—house, but not a welcoming one.

There were no cars in the drive—probably the small courtyard at the left-hand end of the building would have a garage of some sort. The back door would be there as well, handy for the tradesmen's entrance. A house like this would have at least one side door, and possibly french windows.

He rang the front doorbell for a second or two longer than politeness required. With luck it would inject a touch of urgency in the Corners, perhaps even throw them a fraction off balance.

The response was so immediate that it surprised him: a light came on above his head in the shallow porch. The yellow and orange tiles beneath his feet glowed in horrid Technicolor. The destruction of the darkness made him feel more vulnerable. He glanced nervously over his shoulder to see if he was visible from the road.

The door swung open. A dark-haired young woman smiled at him from the threshold. First impressions flooded in: her hair was short, her eyes large and blue, and she had a natural plumpness that appealed to the Major's unashamedly traditional standards of female beauty.

"Good evening. May I see Mr. Corner? They sent me down from the office." He found that second impressions were hastily revising his first. This wasn't a young woman; there were lines around the eyes; glints of silver ran through the dark hair; and the bloom of youth on her complexion was due to the intelligent use of cosmetics.

"My husband's out, I'm afraid. Is there anything I can do?"

Husband? The Major glanced more closely at her, despite the risk of seeming rude. Corner had married Hermione Mary Blacker over thirty years ago. She must be in her fifties now; but she could have passed for late thirties.

The voice was gentle—like Anne's it would be a welcoming voice to come home to. Major Dougal felt a flicker of envy for Corner, which unexpectedly brought with it a glimmer of understanding. If he himself had a wife like this, he would want to keep her happy. Maybe Corner was terrified that the truth about his past could destroy their marriage.

"Can you tell me where to find him?" the Major asked. "I'm so sorry to trouble you, but you know what office crises are like. My name's Harrell, by the way. I have a card." He found the white identity card that Blaines had given him—the one that accredited him to the Ministry of Defense and was intended for official and military consumption; Mrs. Corner must surely have received unexpected callers from her husband's office before.

But she waved away the card when he offered it to her. "It doesn't matter," she told him warmly. "I'm sure you're who you say you are. In any case, I left my reading glasses upstairs."

A lavatory was flushed at that moment, somewhere above their heads. For an instant the Major wondered whether she was lying, to protect her husband from an unwelcome visitor. Then he remembered there was another Corner living at home—the younger daughter, Elizabeth Mary.

Mrs. Corner frowned. "Harry should be at the village hall—they rehearse every second Saturday in the autumn." The frown deepened. "It *is* the second Saturday, isn't it?"

The appeal was launched directly at the Major. He shook his head. "I'm afraid I don't know."

194

"Of course you don't, Mr. Harrell." The frown was replaced with another smile, which dazzled him. "Harry's always saying what a terrible memory I've got." Her eyes veered away from him, as if in search of inspiration. "But of *course* it is," she said excitedly. "Look."

She pointed. Her hand was long and well kept, with a substantial diamond above the platinum wedding band. There was a cardboard box just inside the open door. It contained a couple of sheathed bayonets, a rusting revolver, a peaked officer's cap with a brightly burnished brass badge glowing against the khaki, a battered leather map case, and several neatly rolled belts. Beside the box was a ceremonial sword, leaning against the wall.

"They're props," Mrs. Corner explained. "Harry wasn't sure if they'd be needed tonight." She laughed indulgently. "He's got a whole room full of Great War memorabilia. Between ourselves, he doesn't like lending any of it out unless he really has to."

"His father was killed on the Western Front, wasn't he?" The words were out before the Major could stop them.

"He's mentioned that to you? You must know him quite well. I think that's why he collects this sort of stuff—almost as a sort of memorial to his father. I believe the body was never recovered. He was killed before Harry was even born." Mrs. Corner's expression changed again, as another thought darted into her mind. "I should have offered you a drink or something. You've come from London and—"

"It's very kind of you," Major Dougal interrupted. "But I really should find Mr. Corner. Could you tell me how to get to the village hall?"

Mrs. Corner glowed—no other word was appropriate—with contrition. She had selfishly kept Mr. Harrell chatting here when no doubt all he wanted to do was finish his job for the night and get home. The village hall was just beyond the church on the other side of the road.

As the door closed behind her, Major Dougal felt momentarily bereft. Mrs. Corner might be scatty, but she radiated warmth like a candle flame. He walked down the drive, crossed the road and stared back at the house.

Suddenly everything had become more complicated. It had been easy to envisage dealing with Corner when all he knew of the man were some highly unpleasant actions and a few scrappy biographical details. But meeting Mrs. Corner had fleshed out his knowledge of her husband. He was now a man with hobbies; he had a good marriage and mourned the father he had never known.

There were further complications of a more practical nature. He had been prepared for the risk that Corner's family would see his face; but now it seemed that he would have to make an appearance in the front of the village amateur dramatic society. The odds were lengthening against him in more ways than one.

It took him only a few seconds to reach the village hall. It was a low, red brick building. There was a plaque above the door, explaining that the hall had been erected by public subscription, to commemorate those who had laid down their lives for King and country in the war to end all wars. The formless and faceless dead were listed below.

Major Dougal paused, his hand on the heavy latch. He could hear someone shouting inside the building. It wasn't only the dead who were faceless and formless.

He had no idea what Harry Corner looked like.

20

"IF YOU KILL me now, I am damned." The female with a freckled, discontented face paused before adding conversationally: "I have not been at confession this two years—"

She broke off abruptly and stared at a young man with dark, curly hair, wearing an earring and a pink boiler suit. Petulance gradually spread over her features; she began to tap one foot. The young man looked up.

"Sorry," he said in a thin, pleasant voice. Suddenly he sneered. "When?"

The woman clasped her skinny body somewhere between her navel and breasts. "I am with child," she said defiantly.

"Why then, your credit's saved." The young man gave a thumbs-up sign to a teenager who was scratching his nose and a senior citizen with a pipe in his mouth. They ambled across and strangled the lady; the teenager growled several times to show how nasty he was. Eventually she sat down on the floor, rubbing her neck.

The young man returned to his paperback. "Bear her into the next room." He waggled his forefinger at his two colleagues. "Let this lie still."

The executioners picked up their victim and carried

her a few yards from the center of the stage. The corpse reminded her bearers that she wasn't a wheelbarrow, and thanked heaven she wasn't wearing a skirt.

A tall, portly man with a very red face and an ink-black toupee strode over from the other side of the stage. "Is she dead?" he demanded hopefully.

There was an interruption from the main body of the hall in front of the stage. It came from a fat woman in slacks and a polo-necked jersey. She banged a paperback against the upright piano beside her to gain attention. "Of course she's not dead. Betty dear, can't you try to struggle or something when you're being strangled? Make it a little more convincing?"

The corpse pointed at Major Dougal, who was standing at the back near the door. "He put me off. When someone you're not expecting bursts in, it makes it very hard to die properly." She smiled in his direction. "It's nothing personal, you understand."

"I do beg your pardon." Major Dougal resisted the natural urge to move closer to the people he was speaking to; it was darker at his end of the hall. "Mrs. Corner told me I might find Mr. Corner here."

None of the half-dozen men in the hall gave the instinctive jerk of recognition he was looking for. He had had his hopes of the man with the toupee; even the senior citizen was a possibility.

"He's not here." The man in the pink boiler suit waved his paperback. "That's why I'm reading Bosola. Usually I'm just Delio."

The names acted like the wards of a key turning the tumblers of a lock. A procession of memories passed briskly through the Major's mind: the gritty, merciless heat of a desert summer; that tedious posting to Palestine

198

just after the war; the young National Service subaltern with the unfortunate squint who had lent him a volume of Jacobean tragedies. But he couldn't remember the name of the play or much about it, save that it had been bloody, gloomy, and partially imcomprehensible.

The fat woman walked down the hall toward him. A pair of steel-rimmed glasses swung from a chain around her neck. "Hermione's got her facts wrong," she said with grim satisfaction. "As usual. Harry rang this afternoon to say he wouldn't be able to make it tonight. Most inconvenient."

The corpse chipped in: "He might have let us have the props."

"Oh, Betty." The fat woman sounded exasperated. "You know he'll never let us use his precious relics unless he's here to keep an eye on them." She turned back to Major Dougal. "I don't know what he thinks we'd do with them—give them to the Scouts for their jumble sale?"

The Major felt that some sort of intelligent response was demanded from him. "Ah . . . they seem unusual props for a Jacobean tragedy."

"Exactly." The fat woman beamed at him. "We'll add another dimension to the play. Have you ever heard of a *Duchess of Malfi* with Great War costumes?"

The Major admitted that he hadn't.

"It will link what is essentially a private tragedy with sin, suffering and retribution on a larger scale," she predicted confidently. "There's a terrible tendency to think of the Jacobean dramatists as parochial and elitist, don't you think? We must avoid that at all costs. Even the cardinal will wear the uniform of a British army chaplain. The eight madmen will be shell-shocked tommies."

199

"I'm sure it will be fascinating." Major Dougal abandoned tact. "Did Mr. Corner give you any idea where he was going?"

She shook her head. "He seemed in rather a hurry. Hermione won't know, or rather won't remember. But you could try Liz—their daughter, you know—if she's in. She's been acting as her mother's keeper since she was about six years old."

The Major smiled his thanks, apologized for disturbing the rehearsal and left the hall. As he closed the door softly behind him, he could hear the fat woman demanding a rerun of the murder with a little more anguish from Betty and more dedication on the part of the executioners.

The outside world was perceptibly cooler and darker than it had been five minutes earlier. Major Dougal stepped away from the porch—there was a light over the hall door—and stood in the shadows to consider what he had learned. There were two ways to checkmate a king, he thought: the direct approach, bypassing the royal defences; and the bloodier, less elegant method, which involved destroying those defenses in order to leave the king helpless. After a few seconds he shrugged and walked back up the road, his shoulders hunched against the cold.

The light was still on in the porch of the Old Rectory. He rang the doorbell and waited, bracing himself to face not only the vagueness of Hermione Corner but her insidious charm.

When the door opened, his words of explanation momentarily congealed in his throat. In the last few minutes Hermione Corner had somehow been rejuvenated; she had also shrunk, by several inches, into the pocket edition of her previous self.

200

The illusion shattered as soon as it had formed. This was the daughter, of course. Major Dougal cleared his throat.

"Miss Corner? I'm looking for your father. Mrs. Corner thought he was at the village hall, but I gather he wasn't able to go to the rehearsal."

"That's just like mother." Liz Corner grinned. "It's not so much that she's forgetful, but facts take a while to seep in. No, my father went out this afternoon—he said he might be away overnight. Do you want to leave a message?"

"Oh dear." Major Dougal ran his finger through his hair. He had noticed that the gesture, coupled with a certain expression of his face, tended to arouse the maternal instinct; he found it particularly useful with shop assistants. "It's rather urgent, you see—a problem at work. Is there any way I can get in touch with him?"

As an afterthought he produced the identity card that Mrs. Corner had declined to see. There was something tough and intelligent about this young woman that her mother lacked.

She took the ritual seriously, reading every word and comparing the photographed face with the real one. He watched her covertly, noticing that she wore two ear studs in each ear. How strange young people's notions of adornment could be. The pink tip of her tongue protruded from her lips as she concentrated. She was really young and—like her mother *buxom.*

When she handed back the card, the smile had gone. Her eyes locked on to his. "There's something wrong, isn't there, Major Harrell?"

Major Dougal was genuinely startled. "Why do you say that?"

201

Liz Corner frowned. "Nothing concrete, really. But my father always used to keep work and home apart—you know, nine to five in the office; and when he got off that train the office didn't exist until next morning. They keep a flat for him in town but he could hardly ever bear to use it." She shrugged. "But lately he's been working odd hours; and when he's at home he seems preoccupied. And no one from the office has ever come here before." She blushed, as if suddenly aware that she was thinking aloud—and gossiping about her father to a stranger. But the impulse to go on was too strong for her. "He's meant to be semi-retired."

"I'm afraid I can't comment on that."

"I understand *that.*" Liz's voice was both bitter and resigned. With a shock of recognition, Major Dougal realized that he had heard an identical tone in Anne's voice. It belonged to the families of those on the dragons' payrolls—even, it seemed, to the children of the dragons themselves.

He pushed a little harder, now that he was surer of his ground: "Have you any idea where he is? Or why he went out?"

"There was a phone call after lunch. It was after that he decided to go." She paused and then qualified the statement: "Or rather, I'd heard nothing about him going out before then. My mother went out shopping after lunch, so it's no use asking her. He didn't take any luggage except his briefcase—oh, and he borrowed my road atlas."

The Major clutched at the nearest straw: "Did you see him looking at it?"

Liz wrinkled her forehead. "I think he glanced at it here in the hall. That's right, I remember him saying I'd

202

left the marker in the right place. Then he went off. He took the Ford Granada."

"So you'd left the marker on a particular page. Can you remember which?"

Liz shook her head. "I used the atlas last weekend when I went down to Brighton. But I don't know if I used the marker."

Major Dougal sighed. "Have you made any other journeys recently, using the road atlas?"

"Cornwall in August, of course. And a couple of weekends ago I visited a friend who's just moved to Bury."

"Which Bury? Manchester?" Major Dougal suddenly remembered that vulnerable veteran in the Altrincham nursing home, a few miles from Manchester.

"No—Bury St. Edmunds. In Suffolk." She glanced up at the Major's face and must have seen something there that alerted her. "Does that mean something to you?"

"It might." It could mean far more than he wanted to believe. The possibility lent a nightmarish urgency to what he was doing. He struggled to keep the panic out of his voice. "I've got a few things for your father in the boot off the car. Would you mind giving me a hand with them? I'd like to leave them here."

She walked trustingly down the drive with him. She made him feel like an ogre, in more senses than one; the top of her head hardly reached his shoulders. He stood on the pavement while he fumbled for the keys of the Marina. The dimly lit road was empty, though he could hear the sounds of revving engines from the direction of the village green.

It was one hell of a risk, but it had to be done.

He unlocked the boot and raised the lid with one hand. The other hand dug into the pocket of his jacket and

203

came up with the Browning. He moved sideways against Liz, wrapped his left arm around her and rammed the muzzle of the Browning against her right breast.

"But there's nothing—"

Major Dougal brought his arm up, trapping her mouth in the crook of his elbow. "Get in the boot," he said harshly. "One word and you get a bullet in you. Do as I say and you'll be all right."

Her body went taut against him. Then it began to tremble. He nudged her toward the car and levered her over the rim of the boot. At one point she yanked her mouth free and tried to scream. He cuffed her lightly and slammed down the lid.

He pushed the Browning back into his pocket. The safety catch was on, of course. He expected to hear muffled thuds from the back of the car, but there was nothing. The poor kid must be in shock.

He got into the driver's seat and started the engine. He gripped the steering wheel to stop his hands shaking. *I've grown too old and scrupulous.* He pushed the gear lever into first and drove off up the lane.

After a few yards he realized that not only was he traveling without lights but he was also going in the wrong direction. *Too old.*

The lay-by had caught his attention earlier that evening. It was a mile outside the village. Originally the road had made a dogleg at that point. Now the road had been straightened, leaving the fifty-yard curve of its former course as a lay-by and a means of access to the neighboring fields. The hedgerows had grown unchecked on both sides, shrouding it from the road.

Major Dougal had noted it on the map and briefly reconnoitered it on his way into Reckless. Its existence

204

was—like the size of the Marina's boot—one of the facts he had assembled as possible raw material for future improvisations.

He pulled in and switched on the interior light. He cut two lengths from the nylon rope. He realized that he should have bought luggage ties instead—they would have been both easier to use and more effective. He could use his handkerchief for a gag. Thank God he had taken a clean one today.

The boot lid swung up with a creak. Major Dougal kept well back, the Browning in his hand. He half expected Liz to leap out at him with a tire lever. But she was lying, curled on her side on the floor of the boot. The two huge eyes, dark pools in a ghostly white face, stared up at him.

"Can you breathe in there?" he asked.

She jerked her head in a nod. There was a faint clicking noise: the Major took in the uncomfortable fact that her teeth were chattering.

As he tied her up he talked to her, trying to achieve the difficult feat of simultaneously soothing her and keeping her scared and therefore submissive. The attempt was doomed to failure from the start. When he lifted her, her body flinched away from him. He didn't blame her.

He left her for a moment while he emptied the pockets of his waterproof jacket in the car. She needed the jacket more than he did. It would give her a little warmth and some protection from the bumps. He must remember not to take the corners too fast. *Corners.*

The jacket dwarfed her. He closed the boot and returned to the driver's seat. It was a cool evening, but his hands were clammy with sweat. What sort of a world was it, he wondered, where the sins of the fathers were visited so inevitably upon their children?

21

THE MAN ON the doorstep wore a gray suit that was tightly buttoned over a substantial belly. He looked comfortably plump—the breadth of his shoulders prevented him from seeming fat.

"Is Major Dougal in, please?"

"I'm afraid not." William had one hand on the door and the other on the opposite door jamb. "He's having dinner with friends; I don't know when he'll be back."

Celia was standing in the doorway of the sitting room. William obscured most of the visitor's face, but she could see that he had a full head of silver hair. As she watched, William's back tensed; he dropped his arms and retreated backward into the hall.

Their visitor followed him into the house. "Hands *on* the head, please," he said pleasantly. "You too, Miss . . . Prentisse?" Celia caught a glimpse of a dark, dully metallic shape in his right hand.

He herded them into the sitting room and ordered them to sit on the sofa. He remained on his feet near the fireplace, his eyes ranging round the room. Celia studied him as a rabbit studies a snake. Full, pink cheeks bulged at the sides of his face. The features themselves were unremarkable; there were laughter lines around the eyes, and the mouth, though thin, was gentle. The chin was small and pointed: it protruded with unexpected bony definition from the fleshiness of the jawline.

He tapped the plastic grip of his pistol with a clean, pink fingernail. Celia's vision had sharpened in the last few moments: she could even make out the pearly half-moon at the base of the nail.

"First things first," he said pleasantly. "This is a Walther PPK. The muzzle velocity is nine hundred and fifty feet per second. You can't run faster than that; no one can. The facts add up to a powerful inducement for you to answer any question I care to put to you."

"It would help if we knew who you were," William suggested. He sounded bored, but Celia could see his face had tightened: it was as if his skin had grown too small for his skull.

"You tell me."

"Harold Corner, I suppose. How do you come to be here?"

Corner stared impassively at William. At length he said: "Your tame journalist—Marston, was it?—kept a notepad by his telephone. There were other indications as well, but that clinched it. But let's not talk about me. Tell me what you think you know."

"That you killed my father," Celia said quietly, "and several other people, just to prevent any breath of scandal touching your family and your career. You were scared of two items of buried history; your father was court-martialed, ostensibly for desertion, in 1918; and your uncle killed your aunt in a nasty little domestic murder in 1932. You began to kill earlier this year, when you heard that your Aunt Beatrice was going to talk about the murder on television. You killed my father because he found something that compromised you in an old encyclopedia." She stopped because her mouth was dry, not because she had run out of things to say.

William leaned forward. "How did you hear about Mrs. Hinton and the TV program in the first place?"

"The researchers wanted to dig up the M.o.D. file on John Landis. Naturally I made inquiries. You can imagine my surprise when I found Beatrice was to be their star witness."

"And then what happened?" William asked.

"I sent one of our freelances down to Boreham Hall, pretending to be a journalist. It was quite safe—I took care that there was no direct link between myself and the person in question. Apparently both Beatrice and Miss Bench were very chatty—I imagine a personable young man must have been rather a rarity in that house. In any case, my chap picked up a lot of useful details—like Beatrice's habit of smoking in bed, and the fact that the lock on the kitchen window was broken. The freelance staged the accident a couple of nights later. There is no risk of him identifying me, by the way. I'm just one of several voices he hears on the phone. I gather he believes we're a British branch of the Mafia—"

"And one thing led to another," William cut in brusquely. "As a matter of fact, we wondered if the killing had driven you a little mad. Your murder methods seem too bizarre and finicky to be altogether sane."

Celia sucked in her breath involuntarily. Was William trying to get them killed? But Corner wasn't looking angry—if anything he seemed pleased to have an opportunity to justify himself. She wondered if William was trying to buy time by appealing to Corner's vanity.

Corner stroked the top of the Walther's barrel, as if he was smoothing the ruffled feathers of a captive bird. "I considered the methods very carefully. Each was adapted to the circumstances. Beatrice, for example, died in a way that surprised no one who knew her habits. For Marston I created a neat little contract killing—a perfectly plausible way out for an overinquisitive investigative journalist, though not perhaps a very common one. Variety of method was an important principle for me—murderers who use the same method are the ones who get caught."

"And my father?" Celia asked.

"Naturally you want to know all about that." Corner smiled ruefully. "With hindsight, I think I made it a little too complicated. He found a letter in the encyclopedia, which he could connect with something he already knew—"

"Snowden and Alfred Corner," Celia interrupted.

Corner inclined his head. "Just so. It was quite a shock when he advertised for me. I rang him up and suggested a nice private meeting. Two hundred and fifty milligrams of sodium amytal knocked him out. Then I drowned him." Corner shrugged. "It was all very painless, I assure you."

"But *why?* Why did you have to kill my father? He wouldn't have published anything that he knew would hurt someone."

"I had to be sure." Corner stopped stroking the Walther. "My career and my marriage could both be destroyed if anything got out. I am not exaggerating—the foundations of both of them are delicate." He smiled again. "No doubt a psychologist would say that I'm overcompensating for a loveless and insecure childhood. Perhaps I am: I don't want my daughters to carry the same burden through life as I have had."

For a moment it seemed almost rational to Celia. Then the bubble burst. Corner was pursuing a policy of covering up old scandals with new atrocities; what could only be colossal self-esteem prevented him from realizing that he was heaping up the mathematical odds against himself. More murders increased the chance that sooner or later, one of them would be discovered. Her foreknowledge of the next two murders on Corner's list lay like a dull, inoperable ache in her stomach. Only hatred could partially anesthetize the fear: she thought of her inquisitive, confident father rushing to meet Corner. He would have hated the indignities that Corner had practiced on his body. Most of all he would have loathed being naked.

William coughed and asked if he could have a cigarette. Corner nodded absently. Celia wondered why he hadn't killed them yet. Perhaps his latest tableau of death required the presence of Major Dougal.

Corner's small, shrewd, blue eyes looked directly at her. "I did regret having to kill your father, you know. I have several of his books at home."

"Well, he won't be writing any more, will he?" Celia heard the bitter banality of her reply and wished she could take back the words. Language inevitably cheapened death.

"Tell me, what were you going to do?" Corner's voice had sharpened; he had made the conventional apologies and now it was time to return to business.

William flicked ash into the glass ashtray beside the coffee pot. "Nothing. You must realize that we have no proof. We also know that you are in a position to guard yourself against unsubstantiated accusations."

"When will your father be back? You must have some idea."

"I told you," William said patiently. "I don't know."

210

For the first time Corner betrayed a trace of uncertainty, linked with a hint of irritation. It was ridiculous, Celia thought: he was annoyed because the three of them, his intended victims, had failed to cooperate with the arrangements he had made for their deaths.

William leant forward. "What was the truth about your father? Was he really framed by the authorities because he passed on information to Snowden?" His voice held nothing but casual curiosity but Celia could see what he was doing: he was using delaying tactics and at the same time probing Corner's emotional weaknesses.

Corner looked at him steadily for a few seconds. His face broke into a sudden, unexpected smile. "There's no reason why I shouldn't talk to you about it, is there? I've never been able to discuss it with anyone." The smile vanished. "My father was a socialist. He believed in the Brotherhood of Man." Corner waved the Walther dismissively. "Remember this was nearly sixty years ago. The practical defects of socialism and communism hadn't been apparent by then. And he was a patriot in his way, too. He did supply Snowden with information—he wanted to end the war and the suffering, he wanted to help the ordinary working men he was fighting with. On both sides of the barbed wire. So they framed him. An NCO and a couple of battalion officers did most of the dirty work, but the scheme was conceived and coordinated by military intelligence."

William said in the same even tone: "You can't always have known the truth."

Corner looked away. "When I was really young, I thought he must have been a war hero. Then I was told he was shot as a deserter. I refused to believe it. Now I know he was a hero of a different kind. But the lies have

211

to live on." He shook his great head of hair. "It's always the same: the lies of one generation poison the next."

"Just as your father lied to you," suggested William.

"My father never lied!" Corner snapped.

"Of course he did," William said calmly. "Not to himself, maybe, or to Snowden. But he lied to the army and the whole system of allegiance behind it. He must have lied to his family as well."

"That's absurd." Corner looked pinker than before. "I don't agree with his beliefs—that's part of the problem— but he had every right to live by them as best he could."

The silence prickled with unspoken words. The Walther wavered in Corner's hand. Celia realized that to some degree he must be suffering from shock. It was as if his family skeleton had been entombed in an airtight container. For the first time he had exposed it to the air of public scrutiny; and the brittle bones were starting to crumble.

Her hand slipped gently from her lap onto the seat of the sofa. She could feel the metal rim of the coffee tray.

"You know, of course," William said scornfully, "that your father was in any case a coward? We talked to someone who had served in his company."

The pinkness drained from Corner's face. His eyes seemed harder and bluer than before. He took a step in William's direction. "That's a damned lie—"

Celia's hand curled round the heavy earthenware coffee pot; it was a third full and still warm. She hooked her thumb through the handle and jerked it off the tray.

Corner began to swivel while the pot was in the air, turning from William to her. She was rolling from the sofa to the floor when the gun went off.

There was no pain.

Major Dougal turned off the bypass and drove through Plumford. He had spent much of the journey debating his next move—urgency dictated one course and caution another. As usual he compromised.

He drove slowly up the hill and past his own house. The lights were on in the living room. The only cars on the road belonged to neighbors. For a few blessed minutes he seriously entertained the possibility that he was overreacting. Nevertheless he methodically toured the side roads on either side.

His caution paid off. There was a Ford Granada— either black or dark blue—parked in the second turning on the right up from his bungalow. It might not be Corner's, but he wasn't prepared to take the risk. He noted the registration number.

He parked the Marina even further away in the deserted station car park. If it hadn't been for Liz he would have left it nearer the house. As far as he could tell, she had made no attempt to attract attention during the journey. In the car park—with deserted factories on two sides, a block of offices on the third, and the station itself over fifty yards away—no one could hear any noise she managed to make.

The Browning was on the passenger seat. He picked it up and slid it inside his jacket, holding it in place with his left arm. He locked the car. A few more seconds had to be sacrificed—this time to appease the demands of wholly unprofessional emotion.

Liz was bunched up on the right-hand side of the boot. Her eyes were closed. She gave no sign that she was concious. For a moment Major Dougal feared she might have choked on the gag, or suffocated for want of air in the

213

boot. But when he held his hand over her face he could feel the faint warmth of breath; the hairs on the back of his hand stirred slightly.

He closed the boot as quietly as possible and walked briskly down the hill. The temptation to run was almost irresistible; but he realized he would be of no use whatsoever if he arrived out of breath and with a stitch in his side.

The bungalow was as he had left it. Celia's car was parked outside on the road. Automatically he touched the bonnet: the engine was cold. The heavy curtains had been drawn across the sitting-room window. No convenient chinks of light had been left for passing peeping Toms.

He made a quick circuit of the exterior of the house, keeping on the grass where possible and away from paths. The kitchen light was on at the back of the bungalow. He peered through the crack between the curtains—they had been too small for the window since he washed them last year—but could see no one. The room looked unusually tidy and the door to the hall was closed.

As he had hoped, the top window of the bathroom was open. He hauled himself on to the windowsill and inserted his arm through the gap. The metal handle that opened the lower, larger window was cool to his touch. The window itself moved quietly outwards.

He felt along the tiled windowsill, trying to remember what he kept on there. His fingers came across his razor, shaving mirror, and brush. He picked up each item and gently deposited them on the flower bed.

The bungalow was silent. A thin rectangle of light glowed around the edges of the bathroom door. He clambered over the sill and gently lowered himself feet first onto the seat of the lavatory. His muscles protested against the unaccustomed strain. It must be twenty years since he climbed through a window like this, his own or anyone else's.

His shoulders and his head followed the rest of him into the bathroom. He steadied himself with one hand on the wall, trying to get his breath back before moving off his temporary pedestal. The Browning made a tiny grating noise as it grazed the side of the lavatory cistern.

The door imploded into the bathroom.

The light came on.

As the light came on, someone whispered a single word: *"Freeze."*

William dropped the Walther in the basin and hugged his father for the first time in sixteen years. After a few seconds they stood apart.

Celia was in the doorway. "Oh thank *God.*" She rushed into the Major's arms, narrowly avoiding impaling herself on the barrel of the Browning. "We were so worried."

"So was I." The Major noticed he was sweating slightly and that his hands were shaking. He felt slightly sick. Then the room went dark around him.

He returned to consciousness by degrees. First there was the feel of something cool moving soothingly over his forehead; it was followed by the realization that he was lying on his back on the floor. He thought someone was tickling his cheek with a feather. He opened his eyes and saw Celia's face close to his. Her hair had come loose and trailed on to his face. He smiled weakly.

"So silly. I must have fainted."

Speaking seemed to give him strength. He levered himself up, with a little help from William's arm, until his back was against the side of the bath. William gave him a glass of water. The water reminded him that he hadn't eaten and also brought back his memory. He struggled to get up.

William pressed him down. "It's all right. Corner's in the sitting room and he isn't going anywhere until we decide what to do with him."

Major Dougal allowed himself to relax. For the first time he took in William's appearance. He was paler than usual; there was a nasty gash below his left cheekbone; but his eyes were calm and he couldn't stop smiling. He asked what had happened.

"We realized where you had probably gone, so we decided to spend the evening here. Corner turned up with that Walther. He was rather put out not to find you at home—we think he wanted to find out what we knew and then shoot us all, making it look as it we died because of some suicidal *folie à trois*." William paused and looked quickly at Celia. "Then Celia distracted his attention and we had a little roughhouse. I'm afraid the sitting room is in a bit of a mess. He bashed his head on the gas fire with a little help from me, and then we tied him up. Celia was just going to get some antiseptic"—he touched his cheek lightly and a spot of red appeared on his fingertip—"when she heard someone in the bathroom."

"We'd better check on him," Celia interrupted. "He might have come round, and for all we know—"

"Help me up," said Major Dougal curtly. There was no more time for the luxury of convalescence. William and Celia pulled him to his feet. He picked up the Browning and led the way into the hall.

They advanced cautiously toward the sitting room. The Major, still muzzy after the faint, felt as if he were walking through a nightmare. The watertight seal between his old life at work and his life at home had suddenly ruptured. He was here with a gun in his hand, with his son and his goddaughter behind him; he was creeping down his own familiar hall with that pleasant eighteenth-century print of St. Clement's on his right.

On the threshold of the sitting room his mind cleared. He could smell that a bullet had recently been fired. For an instant he thought the room was both unchanged and empty. But a couple of steps forward allowed him to see the space between the fireplace and the sofa. There was a thickset man half hidden in the deepest armchair. His hands were behind his back: though the position looked uncomfortable, his eyes were closed and he was breathing heavily.

His trousers had been pulled down around his ankles, revealing his muscular, hairy legs and a pair of navy-blue underpants with dashing white piping.

In front of him the hearthrug was strewn with wet coffee grounds and broken glass and crockery. Among the debris was the photograph frame from the mantelpiece.

The Major bent down awkwardly and picked it up. The frame was slightly dented at one corner. He turned it over and saw that the glass was broken. But the photograph itself was undamaged: Anne smiled serenely up at him.

"Corner used it as an offensive weapon after he lost the pistol." William sounded a little embarrassed: an icon remained an icon, come hell or high water. "It was the glass that cut my cheek."

"It doesn't matter." Major Dougal returned the photograph to its proper place. He noticed the bullet hole just above Celia's handbag on the sofa. "Just one shot?"

William nodded and quickly changed the subject. "We tied his hands with shoelaces. I pulled his trousers down to hobble him, not humiliate him; not that I give a damn about his *amour propre* . . . "

The boy was talking too much and too fast, thought Major Dougal. *But he's done a surprisingly professional job—particularly the trousers.*

Celia sat down on the arm of the sofa. "What are we going to do?"

William stopped talking and looked expectantly at him.

The Major said nothing. He walked over to Corner and examined the wound on his scalp. Running his fingers through that thick, wiry hair made him shiver. The skin was hardly broken, and the blood had already dried. A bruise was coming up. He forced Corner forward and checked the efficiency of his bonds.

He turned back to the others. "Come into the hall and I'll explain. We can keep an eye on him from there, and he won't hear us if we talk quietly."

As he moved, the jagged edge of the glass remaining in the frame darted light at him. He stalked out of the room with his shoulders squared. Usually he cherished the hope that somehow Anne might still be in contact with him. Tonight his feeling were reversed: he hoped to God she couldn't see him now.

22

"GET ME THE CARVING KNIFE, will you? And the steel."

William left the room. Major Dougal took a sip of the strong, sweet tea and let the silence grow heavier. Celia was on the sofa, rolling and unrolling the strap of her handbag. Corner sat calmly though uncomfortably in his armchair; his head and shoulders were dripping wet, an aftereffect of William's methods of bringing him back to consciousness.

William returned with the knife and the steel. They had roughened bone handles, worn dark with use. The blade of the knife was now a shallow curve where once it had been a straight line. The carving set had been a wedding present, Major Dougal recalled; but he couldn't remember from whom. The fork and the mahogany box that had contained the set vanished mysteriously during one of those moves that afflicted the life of an army family.

The Major slowly drew the blade down the steel. Gradually he built up a rhythm. He deliberately kept it slow. The slither of metal on metal destroyed the silence.

Corner shifted in the chair. "You're being theatrical, Major." The voice was pleasant but it held a nicely calculated hint of hauteur—a senior official delicately reminding a junior officer under his jurisdiction that there was a natural pecking order in life. The scraping continued. Corner frowned. "I've read your file, you know. There was only one reason why you didn't rise considerably higher, either in the army or later. You're not ruthless enough. One evaluation used the word squeamish. So I don't think you'll be able to treat me like a Sunday joint. Why not drop the pretense?"

Major Dougal replied without breaking his rhythm. "You're making two mistakes." He spoke so quietly that Corner had to lean forward to hear him. "First, when someone's family is threatened, his usual scruples often disappear. You would be the last person to deny that, I imagine. Second, the knife isn't for you, it's in case you need proof that your younger daughter is much nearer to us than Hertfordshire and in much the same position as yourself. I'm afraid she's not quite as comfortable as you are."

"Liz? What have you done to her?" Corner made an effort to control himself: he sat back as far as he was able and his next words were far less vehement. "You're bluffing."

Scrape-scrape; scrape-scrape . . .

"Oh, no. I met your wife too, by the way. She's still at Reckless. I thought you might not believe me. But showing Liz to you would be an unnecessary risk for us. Much easier just to show you her ear. One would do. They cut both the ears off that poor Getty boy, didn't they?"

Corner's nostrils flared but he said nothing. The Major glanced at William and Celia. Their faces were expressionless and neither of them was looking at him. He wondered if they would ever be able to look at him again. He pushed his private life aside: it was time to get back on the job.

220

Scrape-scrape; scrape-scrape . . .

"You might object," the Major continued, his voice sinking almost to a monotone, "that one smallish, well-shaped ear is much like another. So how could you be sure that the severed ear I showed you belonged to Liz? But you and I both know that her ears are pierced—twice in each ear. Not many ears are like that. She was wearing two pairs of studs: one looked like jade and the other could have been jet. An ear with a jade and a jet stud would be pretty conclusive, wouldn't it?"

Corner's pale blue eyes flicked from face to face. He swallowed twice and licked his lips "I—I think I believe you already. I don't need to see an ear, for God's sake. Show me the studs, that's enough."

Scrape-scrape; scrape-scrape . . .

"Very well, William will get them for you in a moment. Before I explain what I want you to do, perhaps you can satisfy my curiosity. What was in that encyclopedia? Where is it now?"

Corner hesitated. "A letter. Can't you stop that damned noise?"

The Major shook his head.

"I burnt it, of course," Corner went on. "My grandmother wrote it to Landis just before his arrest. It more or less accused him of robbing and killing Aunt Muriel, and dragged in my father's court-martial as part of the general muckraking. You knew Landis was concerned in that? I found the letter in the wastepaper basket in his study and tucked it away in the encyclopedia for safety. Then events moved so quickly that I forgot to take it with me when I was sent away. I wish to God I'd known Aunt Beatrice had the encyclopedia all this time. My grandmother told me everything had been sold."

Major Dougal stared thoughtfully at Corner. It all fitted: that damned letter had presented Richard Prentisse with Alfred Corner and the Landis case all in one package. William stirred uneasily but said nothing. The Major allowed the hiatus to lengthen. Corner's eyes flicked to and fro, following the movements of the blade and the steel. The tip of his tongue protruded slightly, just like his daughter's.

"Once you've done what I want," the Major said at last, "Liz will be released."

Corner's eyes jerked up to the Major's face. "How do I know that?" he demanded. "What guarantees can you offer?"

"You're in no position to demand guarantees," Major Dougal pointed out. He felt an unexpected scorn for his trouserless, overweight dragon: Corner was so used to being suspicious that he was failing to see the obvious. "Your best guarantee is that file you've got on me. 'Squeamish' was the word you mentioned; 'not ruthless enough.' I'm not going to kill your daughter unless you force me to. Why should I? She's innocent. She doesn't know who I am or where she is. On the other hand, if your refusal to cooperate puts my own children at risk— not to mention myself—I think I'll be able to overcome my squeamishness. Just this once."

Corner sat in silence for a few minutes, biting his lower lip like a child trying not to cry.

Scrape-scrape; scrape-scrape . . .

"Get the ear studs, would you, William?" The Major glanced toward Corner. "Unless you'd prefer the whole ear?"

There was a moment of silence after the door closed behind William. Then Corner looked up

"You know, Major, I'm not entirely defenseless. There might be something I could do for you."

222

Major Dougal shook his head. "Nothing can alter the position you're in."

"Really? Even your son? I ran a check on him. *Very* interesting."

Celia bit her lip. The Major felt as if he had been kicked in the stomach. All his misgivings—about William's affluence and his unexpected expertise this evening, for example—returned in full force.

"You have a file on him?"

"Let's say that information is available. I gather you haven't seen much of him for about ten years. Let me fill in a few of the more recent gaps. He's spent a lot of time abroad in the last eighteen months. No visible means of support. Special Branch noticed him about a year ago: he was hobnobbing with the rather dubious leaders of a couple of crackpot apocalyptic organizations." Corner paused. "Both of which ceased to exist shortly afterward."

"Is that all?" It was better than the Major had feared.

Corner ignored the interruption. "Known associates include a convicted drug pusher and a distinctly shady Mr. Fixit. You may have heard of the latter—chap called Hanbury? Or was he after your time?" Corner transferred his gaze to Celia. "Earlier this year he spent some time in Virginia—living with a black girl who I'm told is employed by the CIA."

"This is all very interesting." Major Dougal's voice was bored: it was expected when one haggled with dragons. "But I don't quite see what you hope to achieve by it." *Besides the destruction of my peace of mind—and Celia's too, by the look of her.*

"My daughter's safety for your son's," Corner suggested.

"No, no: it won't wash." The Major concealed his relief: Corner's futile attempt to bargain with so small an asset showed how desperate he must be. "It's all rather too hypothetical to be worth worrying about," he lied. "The *possibility* of guilt by association. The *possibility* that William might need your help. The *possibility* that you would be both willing and able to help him. Whereas your daughter's position is anything but hypothetical."

Corner shrugged and relapsed into silence. Major Dougal had little doubt that the man would eventually agree to anything they asked of him: the only difficulty was making sure that he actually fulfilled what he would promise. Family piety was Corner's weakness to the point of obsession—indeed, it was arguably the root cause of these murders—so Liz should certainly make an adequate hostage.

The Major's mind ran ahead, trying to predict Corner's reactions. If he could, he would try to strike back—either to rescue Liz or to take a comparable hostage. It was unlikely that Corner would attack them through William's past—there was no hard evidence; and it could only put Liz into a worse position. But the Dougals, Celia, and Liz would have to vanish until they could be sure that Corner had kept his side of the bargain.

Major Dougal had arranged their disappearance while Corner was still unconscious. All it had taken was a quick telephone call to one of the church wardens of St. Clement's who had a holiday cottage on the north Norfolk coast. It was advertised in the newsagent's as available for short lets. The Major had been to tea there last year: the nearest neighbors, barring sea gulls, were half a mile away and the access road was unmetaled and unsignposted. It would be perfect, both as a a refuge and as a prison. In fact Liz would be far better off there than she

224

would be in that detention center the dragons maintained in Hounslow.

They would have to keep Liz blindfolded, of course. It was a pity she and her mother had seen his face at Reckless. Still, he had taken the precaution of laying a false trail. If they tried to trace the mysterious Harrell from M.o.D., they wouldn't get very far. Harrell was dead; and Colonel Blaines had every reason not to mention his temporary resurrection. The only eventuality he had to fear was the remote possibility of one day running into them by chance: it seemed safe to discount the risk.

Tiredness nibbled at his concentration, but he fought it back. There was so much to do. The hire car would have to go back to St. Albans; and he would have to make his official departure from the Breakspeare Arms and pick up his own car. It would be politic to ring Margaret and postpone their evening together. He must remember to turn off the water and cancel the milk—

The front door slammed. William strode into the sitting room, taking the Walther from his jacket pocket. His other hand was balled in a fist.

"She's okay, considering everything." He smiled at Celia, who stared blankly back. "I took her a blanket."

He opened his hand and Celia gave a little gasp. On his palm were the ear studs, one black and one green—and also a tuft of black hair.

Corner blinked rapidly, three times, and cleared his throat. "What exactly do you want me to do?"

Major Dougal ran his finger along the blade of the carving knife. Suddenly he felt overwhelmingly weary; his eyes might have been rimmed with lead.

"I want you to commit the perfect murder."

Epilogue

HARRY CORNER DERIVED a certain pleasure from the planning of the perfect murder. The conception behind it, though not his own, was undoubtedly elegant. Nevertheless, he had tried to avoid the need for it. But Major Dougal and his entourage had disappeared before he could put a trace on him. And Liz, he could only presume, had gone with him.

The two ear studs, one jade and one jet, had lived in his waistcoat pocket ever since. Oddly enough he could distinctly recall having an argument with Liz when she arrived home with the second pair of holes pierced in her ears.

He was not surprised that Major Dougal had vanished. The man was too intelligent to leave open such an obvious countermove. In a twisted way, Harry was even grateful to the Major. The twilight uncertainties were gone; everything was now black or white.

If Harry committed the perfect murder, Liz would go free and the secrets in the lives of her father and grandfather would remain permanently undisturbed.

If he didn't, Liz would die, his family would be destroyed, and the lies and crimes of the past would be exposed.

He hadn't slept for two days; on the third he would sleep forever.

Major Dougal was the murderer; Harry Corner was both instrument and victim.

He remembered four lines that the Duchess of Malfi had often said to him in rehearsal:

> *I know death hath ten thousand several doors*
> *For men to take their exits; and 'tis found*
> *They go on such strange geometrical hinges,*
> *You may open them both ways . . .*

He would open his door from inside. But which door? The Major had stipulated only that he should die. Harry could make his own choice of exit. Suicide was the obvious one, but there were two reasons why Harry preferred not to commit suicide. It would hurt Hermione and the children—the former particularly, because her father had committed suicide. Suicide would also invalidate his life insurance policy. If Hermione had to live without him, she should at least be able to do it in comfort.

His death therefore needed to seem either murder or accident. The former would be easy to arrange: he could simply put a contract on himself; it would entail nothing more than a couple of phone calls and a visit to the bank. But there would be two problems with this. Contract killers could not be relied upon to do an efficient, painless job. Moreover, if a man in Harry's position were murdered, too many people would want to know why. A thorough investigation could uncover the very facts he wanted to keep concealed.

But how did one kill oneself in such a way that it seemed like an accident? The question obsessed him as he drove back to Reckless on Saturday night. It stayed with

227

him as he sat awake through the hours of darkness in the heavy leather armchair in the room that was both a study and a shrine to the memory of his father. It was there at breakfast time, when Hermione was chattering away about the difficulties of getting free range eggs, even though there were three farms on the Old Rectory's doorstep. She had cooked two for Liz, forgetting that he had told her, when he brought up her early-morning cup of tea, that their daughter had gone down to Brighton on impulse last night, to spend a few days with the latest boyfriend.

After breakfast he retired to the study, ostensibly to read the Sunday papers. Instead he waited for phone calls that never came and contemplated those of death's exits that were open to him. Death itself did not disturb him. He saw it as an end to existence, rather than a transition to another one. Nothing could disturb him once he was dead. But the process of dying was another matter. He wanted no pain. An overdose of morphine to the accompaniment of a Mozart divertimento tempted him severely; but for Hermione's sake he couldn't allow himself the luxury.

He worried intermittently about Liz and, to a lesser extent, about the rest of his family. How could they manage without him? At least his affairs were in good order. And this time, no documentary evidence would be left behind to disturb future generations. He had already destroyed almost all the papers from the file Prentisse had brought with him to their meeting.

He should have burned the one exception long ago, as soon as Prentisse had drifted off into his coma. But it was of sentimental value to him, for many reasons. It was his manifesto; it was also the one piece of the puzzle that had eluded Major Dougal—and perhaps the most significant of them all. It was fortunate that the Major had accepted that invention of a letter from Granny.

Hermione roasted a chicken for lunch, along with succulently gilded potatoes. Harry ate well—there had never been anything wrong with his digestion, unlike Aunt Muriel's—and now there was no longer any need to worry about the thickening waistline. Hermione unwittingly provided the answer to his problem while he was eating his second helping of lemon syllabub.

"Darling, you couldn't have a look at my car sometime today, could you? The engine's terribly noisy at present."

The next few hours passed quickly. It was one of those long autumnal afternoons with colors so vivid they seemed to belong to another time and another country. Harry suggested a walk; he would look at the car later.

Soon after they returned, Jane—their elder daughter—phoned to announce that the Corners' first grandchild had just produced his first tooth. The baby himself was brought to the phone and burbled in his private language to his grandfather.

The Corners had a light supper; Harry drank rather more than usual during and after it. After coffee, Hermione decided to go to bed—the fresh air, she said, must have tired her out. Harry was not surprised: he had ground up two Mogadons and added them to her coffee. As a rule, he himself needed little sleep; and Hermione saw nothing unusual in his decision to tinker with her car before going to bed.

He kissed her good night outside the bathroom door. For ten minutes he wandered round his study, touching his possessions. He picked up a cassette and the last paper that needed to be destroyed, and stood for a moment outside their bedroom door. There were no sounds inside; the light was off; and in any case the room faced away from the garages.

The golden afternoon had given way to an evening of blustering rain. Under the shelter of an umbrella, Harry splashed out to the stableyard. The old loose boxes had been converted into three garages, each self-contained and with its own swing door.

The weather made it plausible that he should close the door behind him once he was inside. Hermione would tell them later—if of course she remembered—that he had had two large brandies after supper and most of a bottle of claret with it; they would assume him to have been not entirely sober.

Hermione's dark blue Triumph Spitfire stood waiting for him. She had bought it new eleven years ago, and treated it ever since as a sort of four-wheeled family pet. She resisted all his attempts to interest her in a more practical car.

Harry lifted the bonnet and glanced at the exhaust manifold. The gasket had gone again. Leaving the bonnet up, he climbed into the car, folded back the hood and started the engine. He fed the tape into the cassette deck; but unfortunately the noise of the engine in that confined space all but drowned the delicate music. The perfect murder would have to be marred by the absence of Mozart.

The low-slung seat was comfortable. He angled it further back and allowed his head to be cushioned by the headrest. It would look as if he had started the car to get an idea of the trouble his wife had mentioned; he had dozed off in an alcoholic postprandial haze, leaving the engine running; and the carbon monoxide had done the rest. They would try to comfort Hermione with the information that he had almost certainly fallen asleep and died without pain. Harry hoped their information would be correct.

The carbon monoxide would fasten on to the hemoglobin in his blood, displacing the oxygen as a cuckoo pushed out the rightful occupants of a nest. His skin would eventually turn cherry red. But, long before that, he would be asleep.

In any case, fatigue, alcohol, and even relief were conspiring to send him to sleep before the carbon monoxide could do its work. Suddenly he jerked awake. The paper was still in his pocket.

He struggled out of the car. There was a box of matches on the windowsill, along with a candle. Hermione had a dread of power cuts. He took the sheet out of his pocket and unfolded it. It was a lined page from an exercise book, yellowed by age. The spidery writing was a rusty brown color.

Harry smiled. He still had a tiny scar on his left arm, self-inflicted with a penknife when he was thirteen. It had been surprisingly difficult to get enough blood for his purpose, and to use it before it clotted. But the melodrama reinforced the significance of the gesture. The next day he had made his first experiment.

The paper was in places smudged with gray where it had sucked ink from the pages of the encyclopedia that had kept it secret for half a century. The faded writing was still legible.

I, Harold J. Corner, hereby swear vengeance through all eternity on those who have calumniated the memory of my dead father, Alfred Xavier Corner. Chief among these are

my Aunt, the abominable Muriel Hinton, and my Uncle,
the betrayer John Landis. They say he was a liar, a spy, a
deserter. He was a hero. They are the liars, and they shall
die for it. They try to kill his memory with words. I shall
kill them both in fact. Then they will rot in Hell together.
Signed,
H. Corner.

With one swift movement he crushed the paper into a ball. He held a match to one edge and watched as the yellow triangle of flame grew larger. When the paper was too hot to hold, he let go. The fireball fell gently to the floor. Harry nudged it twice with his foot to keep it alight. There was a certain grim satisfaction in the thought that the flame was devouring oxygen as well as paper: his life was shortening before his eyes.

Only ashes were left. He ground them into the concrete with his heel. The garage floor was so stained that no one would notice it. He returned the matches to the windowsill and got back into the car.

His eyes closed. His mind drifted back to that first murder, the one secret that would never be uncovered. For an instant he wished he could have told Major Dougal about it. It would have been a relief to tell someone how it felt to be a poor relation in that house in the Fens, deprived of the one consolation open to him, his father's memory. He had found the arsenic by chance in the shed. At first he hadn't really thought it would kill Aunt Muriel—that would have been too good to be true, like a direct answer to prayer.

But a little bit here and there, in her food and drink, had produced such instantly gratifying results. The tyrant was humbled, her head bent low over a chamber pot. And no one suspected, even that slimy little doctor.

So Harry had continued to dose his aunt. He hated her, and he was curious to see what would happen. In recent years he had wondered whether intellectual curiosity was an unrecognized ingredient in the psychology of murder; a successful murder bore many similarities to a daringly conceived but ultimately successful scientific experiment.

He cried when he was told of her death. Muriel's death was devoutly to be desired; but death itself came as something of a shock. Afterward events had moved out of his control. It was as if the Angel of Death had decided to take a personal interest in the justice of his cause. Harry had intended to do something about John Landis but, when the time came, there was no need. Fate and Uncle John had done his work for him.

John Landis's greed for Muriel's money had ironically supplied most of the circumstantial evidence that convicted him for her murder. Harry hadn't expected Muriel's death to be treated as murder but, when it was, he had seized his chance. It was he who had placed the arsenic in Muriel's decanter and in the chair in Uncle John's study. He had had the sense to exercise restraint. There was no point in taking unnecessary risks. As it was, no one would suspect a child when there was an adult male with a strong motive available.

Harry's chuckle turned into a yawn. He could feel the lethargy drifting over him. In a while no more lies would be necessary. He would no longer be a husband or a father. He rubbed his forehead: the fumes were giving him a headache.

Sleep drew him nearer. At one point he stopped and glanced back toward consciousness. There was a half-formed thought in his mind: perhaps William Dougal was right—if Alfred Corner hadn't lied, would Harry Corner

233

at this moment have been sliding into bed beside his wife?

The thought was ugly. He dismissed it, turning back toward sleep and accepting the tug of oblivion with relief.

His last conscious thought was a pleasant one: *If there was any question why I died, there would be . . . no . . . answer.*